Student of Kyme

A Wraeththu Mythos Novel

Student of Kyme

A Wraeththu Mythos Novel

Storm Constantine

IMMANION PRESS
Stafford England

http://www.stormconstantine.com

Cover Design by Storm Constantine
Cover Art by Ruby
Alba Sulh map by Andy Bigwood
Edited by Fiona McGavin
Set in Souvenir

IP0016
An Immanion Press Edition
8 Rowley Grove
Stafford ST17 9BJ
UK

http://www.immanion-press.com
info@immanion-press.com

ISBN 978-1-904853-41-1

The Calendar of Wraeththu

January - Snowmoon
February – Frostmoon
March - Windmoon
April - Rainmoon
May - Flowermoon
June - Meadowmoon
July – Ardourmoon
August - Fruitingmoon
September - Harvestmoon
October - Vintagemoon
November - Mistmoon
December – Adkayamoon

Monday – Lunilsday
Tuesday – Miyacalasday
Wednesday – Aloytsday
Thursday – Agavesday
Friday – Aruhanisday
Saturday – Pelfazzarsday
Sunday – Aghamasday

Nunavut Territory

Realm of the
Ice Striders

Freygard

Freyhella

P

H — N

E

Wundles teeth

Scorpio

Tuaththua

Oorn Islands

Cantesua

Midphan-jortgard

Hand's teeth

Alba
Phorlakhan

Lyonessua

Hacele channel

The Skage

The Girdle
of Tiamat

The Great
Divide

Gilly

The Isle of Towers

Lir Alba

Deep Solice

Linvallas

By'Fayganza

Alba Sulh

Yorvick

Kredge

Sentavoi

Isle of Men

Kyme of the Great Library

Tiamaton

Alba Keltoi

Porthwallas

Ijhimere of the
Green Heart

Calme

Great Wall of Lund

Ruin of The
Lund

The Emerald Lir

Avalona

The Old
Places

Sulh Jinh

Shadowvale

Lyonis

Cal'sulh

The Realms of
The Sulh

Jesith

Studlun on Drift

The Little Divide

The Veridian
Tapestry

Cordagne

Bright Mornaandai

Introduction

We must be thankful for all lessons that life bestows upon us. In grief and hardship, in pain and conflict, lies education of the highest order. When we can rise above ourselves and affirm our tragedies, so we grow more into our potential. Weep not in the moment, but face towards the future, when you can look back and see the lesson for what it was.

Aghama gives to us that which we need; everything we experience is for our highest good, even if it does not seem so at the time of tears. We simply have to be wise enough to realise the truth of it.

Velisarius har Kakkahaar, from 'We Who Are Stars' ai-cara 120

I began this account a long time ago, and reached a point with it when I could no longer continue. It was simply too painful. The quote above is set there for a reason. It was only later, after I had moved to Immanion and worked there for some time, that I found the heart to finish it. And the Tigron Pellaz himself is partly responsible for that.

There is great store set upon the fact that Wraeththu are superior to humankind, but the truth of it is that we have the *potential* to be greater. We derive from humanity, and even those of us who proudly call ourselves 'pure born' or 'second generation' still carry within us the material of our forebears. There have been great conflicts in our short history, many dramas enacted upon the stage of the world, and it is these that scholars use as illustrations in their discourses on how we can progress as a species. But to me, the smaller conflicts are

9

just as important. While tribes might clash, and the lessons learned from these wars be world-changing, our personal battles are of equal value. These are the dramas we encounter in everyday life, in our small corners of the world; in work, in play, in love.

After a silence of years concerning these very intimate matters, I spoke with Pellaz har Aralis, simply because I knew he had firsthand experiences of the destructiveness of love. In the summer, I had been lucky enough to attend a gathering at the palace Phaonica with my employers, and near the end of the evening found myself in a group with the Tigron himself. We were sitting on a wide balcony overlooking the city. I remember the smell of the night, the heady perfume of night blooming jasmine, and for some reason it took me back a few years. In my head and my heart, I was in Alba Sulh again, smelling flowers that had died long since. Thoughts weighed heavily upon my mind, and I found myself wondering whether it is possible ever to forget.

Gradually, for one reason or another, the company drifted away, until it was just Pellaz and I sitting there. I did not feel uncomfortable; he has a way to put you at ease.

'What's on your mind?' he asked me.

'Oh, nothing important,' I replied, embarrassed my wistfulness had been so obvious.

He laughed softly. 'Why not tell me the truth?'

I realised then he was probably the best har to speak to about it. His history was common knowledge, because he was one of the most famous hara in the world. Therefore, he was allowed few secrets.

'I was just thinking back,' I said. 'I was thinking... I was thinking of a lost love.' I shook my head. 'Why do I still dwell on it? It is a long time finished. I've worked very hard to rise above it all, create my life as I want it to be, yet still the memory steals upon me sometimes.' I grimaced. 'It still feels like a battle I did not win.'

Again, Pellaz laughed, louder this time. He said to me, 'Never doubt it *is* a war, but perhaps the trick is to discern who the combatants really are. Is it you and another, or is it simply parts of yourself: one the wiser self, the other a mean little sneak sabotaging all its better's plans and intentions? Our goal in life is to understand ourselves, nothing more, nothing less, because all other work and progress springs from that endeavour.' Then he smiled at me. 'Just write it down,' he said. 'It's what I did. You'll find it helps.'

Pellaz wasn't the first to give me that advice, but he was the har who gave me the courage to complete the work. The account that follows was begun at the start of my time in Kyme. I finished it last night.

Gesaril Har Sulh

Lunilsday, Flowermoon 7

Kyme is a town that has never been young. Even when humans lived in it, I know that the dust of antiquity swallowed their dreams and muffled up their memories. It's not that I don't like it here, I do, but it's a strange, heavy place. I've been here four days and it feels like being in prison, even though I can go out if I want to. Codexia Huriel has given me a room in his house, and it's very dark and creepy. The furniture is old, the floorboards slope, and there are noises in the walls after dark. Every time I get into the bed it makes a single long groan, then never speaks again all night.

Huriel has told me I must write about my experiences, and that this is part of the healing process, but I can't think of anything to say about it all just now. I don't even want to think about it, but no matter how much I say that to myself, it consumes my every waking moment. I am haunted, and maybe I'll always be haunted. Nohar else can see the ghost, and it doesn't stand at my shoulder; it's some distance away, but always at the edge of my vision. I know: I sound insane. So perhaps writing about it will be an exorcism. I'll start my story, if story it is, just before the journey here.

Huriel interviewed me in Jesith, in the phylarch Sinnar's office, although Sinnar wasn't there. I didn't know what to expect from the Kymian, and I know I was pretty defensive. I could tell he thought I was a brat. Sometimes, these words just come out of my mouth, and there's a voice in my head yelling at me to stop, but it does no good. So I bratted the poor har for over an hour, and we didn't get anywhere. I didn't know what was going to happen to me, whether I'd be punished or seen as mad, whether I'd be sent home or on to another teacher. My time in Jesith was over, I knew that. Hara believed I'd fouled everything. Really quite disgusting. My parents had sent me there to get an education, but I'd simply gone faintly insane and acquired a bad reputation instead. Part of me hated myself, another part felt indignant, because it really wasn't all my fault. But nohar would believe me. It was my word against that of a har who was greatly respected around these parts. I was in so much pain, I couldn't even feel it any more. All I could do was scratch and spit; it was my shout against the injustice I felt.

'Your future is really up to you,' Huriel said to me patiently.

His patience especially infuriated me. 'What do you mean?' I snapped.

He placed his hands on his crossed knees. 'Well, you can go home if you wish, or continue your education.'

I laughed. 'Or you could lock me up.'

'What is your choice?' Huriel enquired. I noticed with gratification that his teeth were gritted.

I shrugged. 'Whatever.'

Huriel breathed out through his nose. He wanted to be any place but in that room with me. 'We know about your problems,' he said, 'and, to be frank, in your position I would want to address them and move on. It's clear you need supervision, and I suggest you come back with me to Kyme.'

Again, I laughed. 'What's wrong with you? Don't you know what I'm capable of?'

He fixed me with a look that said so much. I lost about half of my swagger in an instant. 'You will be quite... *safe* with me.'

'You don't want to do this, so why bother?' I said. 'Will your charity make you feel good?'

'I hope so,' Huriel replied dryly, again saying so much more than the simple words implied. He got to his feet. 'Well?'

I thought for a moment about going home to the Shadowvales, and my willowy father drooping all over me, asking why I'd come back. I thought of my hostling, who is so far away with the fairies, I swear the concept of reality is less real to him than dreams. Whatever might happen in Kyme, it had to be more tolerable than that. My skin itched all over. I felt fierce and restless. 'All right,' I said. 'But I've addressed my *problems*, as you put it. What can I do in Kyme?'

'Continue your training, but in a more academic manner,' Huriel said, gathering up his notes. 'I have a lot of old texts I'm working through. You could help me with that. I could do with an assistant.'

'Will you continue with my caste ascensions?'

He nodded. 'It's desirable for hara of our community to advance,' he said. 'The library at Kyme is the biggest resource in Alba Sulh. We're called upon by phylarchs for our knowledge and expertise. We undertake magical commissions, and offer education. Under the circumstances, your phyle will not be charged for your education.'

And that was that.

The next day, we began the long journey north. There was no har for me to say goodbye to, and we left Jesith just after dawn. All the previous night, I'd lain awake wondering whether my erstwhile teacher would come to me, at least to say farewell. (I can't even write his name yet, not without flinching away as if from a blow.) I wondered whether I should leave a note for him; an apology or an embittered rant. I wrote so many of them in my head. There was a sick sticky lump where my heart should have been. He probably wasn't even thinking of me. So, as my horse followed Huriel's from the town, I didn't look back once, didn't think. I looked ahead.

Huriel didn't like me, and it was impossible to use my wiles on him. He was faintly attractive to me – I liked his dark auburn hair – but I might as well have been a rat he'd picked up by the tail from a rubbish dump for all the attention he sent my way. He clearly thought his immense wisdom and experience was way beyond my ability to comprehend. He barely took care to guard his thoughts and on one occasiononce I picked up the impression he considered my head to be full of air. He just hoped I was capable of putting things in alphabetical order. Strangely, none of this offended me. I quickly realised his non-attention was actually a relief. Usually, the looks hara give me make me light up like a flaming torch, and I become this *thing* that sort of smoulders and claws. Sometimes, I really don't want to do that, but I just can't help it. My dreamy parents cursed me with beauty, but Huriel wasn't impressed by it. I was glad for this change. It meant I could be myself – my real secret self - and be quiet. We hardly conversed at all.

The dehara who organise the weather must have looked kindly upon us, because the cold spring rain kept away. I enjoyed seeing new places. As we moved further away from Jesith, the pulsating hurt inside me would sometimes fade a little. I found balm in the raw landscape. Occasionally, moments passed when I did not see *his* face before my inner eyes, when the wound where my heart used to be didn't hurt quite as much; but these were temporary respites. One time, as I watched a hawk hovering high in the cold blue sky, I realised that I

Student of Kyme

had no idea how long it would take to recover from this
grief I felt, or if I ever would recover. I still feel that way.
Is grief to be my constant companion now? I just can't
imagine life without this hungry ghost.

Whenever Huriel and I stopped for the night in a
town or village, hara would look at me with interest, but
their sensual glances merely annoyed me. I was feeling
very peculiar. Once, perhaps noticing this, Huriel steeled
himself with obvious great effort and asked if I 'needed
anything'. I knew what he meant, but said, 'Like what?'

'Do you want to take aruna?' he asked, deadpan.

I laughed. 'With you? Do you want to with me?' I
knew the answer to that, of course, but even so I enjoyed
his discomfort.

'Gesaril, I would rather eat my own tongue, if you
must know. Do you need to or not?'

'You're too romantic for me,' I replied. 'Don't worry,
I can contain myself.'

'Is there still a *problem*?' Huriel asked, a triumph for
him, since the words made me go cold and awkward.

'No,' I answered. 'I'm enjoying being alone for a
while, that's all. Surely even you can understand that,
given my *problem*.'

He nodded once. 'Good. I've taken on the task of
being your mentor. Regardless of our opinions of each
other, you must approach me if you have any needs, or
want advice. I hope you feel you can speak to me.'

'Of course,' I said. 'You've been very open and
welcoming.'

He didn't respond to that.

We came into Kyme from the west, and I loved it at
once. It was so full of atmosphere, sort of brooding and
mysterious, far darker than the Shadowvales, where I'd
grown up. I liked that aspect. Life in the Shadowvales is

17

often like wallowing in sweet marshmallow. I sensed a whiff of threat in Kyme, as if ancient resentful spirits lurked in the hanging eaves of the buildings.

Huriel lives in what I suppose was once a grand town house owned by rich humans. It has a courtyard in front of it, stables, and a large garden at the back. He'd told me he was part of the inner cabal of the Library Codexiae, close to Malakess, the High Codexia himself. Huriel is very smug about his good connections. Anyway, he let me wander around the house and pick a room for myself from the seven that were available. I didn't choose the biggest or the airiest, but a middle sized room right at the top of the house, on the third storey, which has a sort of haunted feel to it. I wonder why I like that, seeing as I've so recently got rid of a haunting that scared the wits from me (and I'm not talking about the haunting of love). But I've seen no real ghosts yet, despite the scratching sounds in the walls, and the room feels like mine. I lie on the bed alone for hours, just dozing. I don't want to think, because all the wrong thoughts pop out, but how can you stop yourself when your brain is so active? I don't want faces in my head, but his is there before me constantly. He is so strange-looking. I really don't know why he affected me the way he did. It's an aura he has. It's like a flame, and other hara lie around his feet like insects burned to crisps, drawn to the light only to perish within it. I realise now that part of me really is dead, as surely as if he'd taken a knife to it with his own hand. I am angry because he made me out to be a liar, a delusional fool and a manipulative schemer. Perhaps I am those things in some ways, but I was not alone in what happened between us. It is not fair I was made the scapegoat. Yet even knowing this, I can't find it in my heart to hate him. If I had friends, they'd say to me that time will heal everything and I'll get over it and forget about him. Can this be true? How can it be possible to feel this way and then for it all simply to disappear? I hope it is true. I really do.

Now, I am tired. I have exhausted myself with feeling. I kneel upon the wide windowsill, my cheek pressed against the glass. I look two minutes into the future. My hands in my lap look too thin, too vulnerable. My notebook lies open and I can see that one of my hairs has fallen down and lies curled there on the page half filled with writing. Once he put his hand upon my hair, and he said to me that he would always be there for me. Now I am alone. Two minutes into the future. I will put down my pen.

Aloytsday, Flowermoon, 30

Yesterday, I got such a horrible shock, it's inspired me to start writing again. I haven't done any for about three weeks, because to be honest, I haven't felt like I've had anything to say. The thought of writing more about pointless longing just tires me out and I can't be bothered.

I haven't seen that much of Kyme yet, because I tend to stay around the house and garden. It's such an old place, and the atmosphere comforts me. It's like going into a 'no place', where nothing else exists. There's a walled orchard I like and I go there every morning, just to sit on a mossy old stone bench and listen to the birds. In the distance, I can hear the sounds of hara going about their lives. I want to be like them, do normal things, think normal things or else not think at all.

Huriel has put me to work, and I actually quite enjoy it. Huriel changes when he's among old books. Some of his haughtiness goes away. He's glad I'm interested in his work. Malakess has given him the task of transcribing some very old human works on the occult and ceremonial magic. I love the old fashioned words and like to read them aloud. I think Huriel likes to hear them too. He doesn't hate me as much now, because I've been behaving myself. He has a staff of two hara – Ystayne and Rayzie - who cook and clean the house. They seem all right, although they're wary of me. I don't know how much hara in Kyme know about me, or how I nearly ruined one of the most respected hienamas in the country. Because I think they're thinking bad thoughts about me, I don't want to speak to them, but I might be wrong.

I now have almost a pleasant friendship with Huriel, and we've got a pretty boring daily routine, but it makes me feel secure, so I'm not complaining. Life is slow and regular. We've agreed to leave my caste ascension work until I've settled in some more.

Sometimes, I can go for hours at a time and not think about my nemesis. I never thought I'd write those words and mean them. I sent a letter to my parents, again not sure how much the hara in Jesith might have told them, but explaining that my education had taken a turn for the better, and I'd been taken on by none other than a Codexia of Kyme. I talked about the books, which I know won't interest my parents at all, and described how wonderfully dark and strange Kyme is. They won't like that either. If something doesn't emanate light and loveliness, my parents tend to put their hands over their ears, shut their eyes, and start humming loudly.

But, on to my shock...

High Codexia Malakess spends a lot of time in Almagabra, fraternising with the Gelaming, and making plans for the world. From what Huriel's told me about him, I couldn't help imagining him as looking like some kind of human wizard with a long grey beard or something. I know that's ridiculous, but the idea of him just oozes fustiness and old age, as in pictures I've seen in some of Huriel's books: serious men pointing at arcane instruments of alchemy, not looking at one another, their postures stiff and graceless. Anyway, yesterday morning at breakfast, Huriel said that Malakess was back in Kyme and coming to visit. He wanted to discuss with Huriel his recent meetings.

'Do you want me to make myself scarce?' I asked.

Huriel frowned. 'No. Just don't get in the way or be impertinent. Do you think you can manage that?'

'I've been perfectly good, as you well know!' I said.

Huriel's frown changed to a smile. 'I know. I have noticed. You might be bored though. Perhaps you should finally go out and about a bit. Take the day off.'

I realised, by the cold feeling that went through my stomach, that I might be developing a phobia about the outside. 'I don't mind working.'

'Gesaril,' Huriel said sternly. 'I get the impression you really *should* go out.'

He could read my mind, I suppose. 'Oh, all right, then.'

We hadn't even finished breakfast when somehar knocked at the front door. One of Huriel's staff went to answer it, and then conducted the visitor to the dining room. I looked up from the remains of my meal, saw him, and the cold inside me turned to ice. Ysobi har Jesith was standing at the threshold. (There: his name). It was like some hideous ghost. He was very tall, more so than hara tend to be, with the same bony-faced attenuated appearance. The impression lasted only a moment, but even so, it hit me like a punch to the stomach. Hara were talking, but I couldn't hear anything. Eventually, the sound of my name penetrated my trance. 'Gesaril... Gesaril!' It was Huriel. 'This is High Codexia Malakess. Where are your manners?'

'I'm sorry,' I blurted, physically incapable of looking at that har again. 'I feel ill. Excuse me, tiahaara.'

Almost blind, I lurched from my chair and ran from the room. I fled to my own room, threw myself on the bed, and erupted into a fit of weeping. I realised, with horrible sick despair, how much I was still in love with Ysobi, no matter how I'd tried to squash all the feelings flat, fold them away and close the lid on them. How could life be so cruel? Why did it have to throw this har who looked like Ysobi in my path? Malakess har Kyme.

Not a grey beard in sight. He was beautiful to me.

Huriel came to find me only minutes later. No doubt he'd been embarrassed having to explain to his great teacher that he'd taken on a lunatic like me. 'What on earth's the matter with you?' he asked me.

'Nothing,' I said. Pathetic.

'You look like you saw a ghost down there. What was it you saw in Malakess?'

Couldn't Huriel see it himself? He knew Ysobi well, and had trained him here in Kyme. I thought the similarity was obvious, and certainly didn't want to say it. An inventive fiction was in order. 'I'm sorry, Huriel. I must have embarrassed you. The fact is, I think I've got a problem about going out. I was thinking about it when Tiahaar Malakess arrived, and it made me feel physically sick.'

Huriel sat down on my bed and folded his arms. 'We'll have to do something about that.'

I nodded. 'Yes... I really am sorry. Ag knows what it must have looked like, me running out like that. I thought I was going to vomit.'

'Stay up here for a while,' Huriel said. 'Calm down. Then go into the garden, take some air. Perhaps you'd feel better going beyond the grounds with somehar else. We'll talk about it with Ystayne and Rayzie.'

'Do we have to?'

'There are no secrets in this house,' Huriel said. 'They're good hara. They'll help you.'

He patted one of my legs and then left me.

I curled onto my side, and I swear I could smell Ysobi's personal scent around me. Morning sunlight came in through the window, filtered green by the Virginia creeper that had stretched tendrils over it. The day was so beautiful and mellow and there I was, remembering the way Ysobi used to smile at me, how he was always so pleased when I got something right in my caste work, because I could be such a nasty petulant thing and liked to annoy him by not working. When I did something well, he saw it as an achievement for both of us. Back then, in those days when I had begun to see him as more than a teacher, I thought he had exorcised the ghosts of my past, but in fact he'd invoked them. He'd opened me up, as if I was spread-eagled on a dissecting board, and had started fiddling around with my insides. He didn't know about my past, of course. I didn't tell him, when I should have done.

Curled in on myself, I tried to banish the image of Ysobi's face from my mind. I wept because I knew I could never see him again. He had a chesnari, who had fought for him and won. Once Ysobi had truly realised what I'd felt for him, he'd acted horrified and had backed off, even though he'd been responsible, for the most part, for making me feel that way. I know he'd wanted to make me love him but once he'd achieved that, it became a nuisance, so he'd abandoned me without a second thought. Jassenah, his divine consort, had been free to gloat. I wonder if they ever talk about me? If so, it's probably to laugh. I was just a harling to them, and a messed up one at that. Their pity would be worse than their scorn. Why, why, why did my stupid parents send me to Jesith?

Such thoughts are pointless. It is torture. Love is a vile thing. It's a disease. I'm still infected, but once I'm over it, and I've decided I *will* get over it one day, it'll never ever happen again.

Later

After an hour or so, I felt stable enough to go back downstairs and out into the garden. One of the staff, Ystayne, was out there, kneeling on the lawn next to the herb bed, cutting some sprigs for lunch with a pair of tiny silver scissors. He was so precise about it. It made me feel warm inside for some reason. I wandered over to watch him and he glanced at me over his shoulder. 'I heard you had a fit at breakfast.'

'Hmm, yes,' I said. 'I'm scared of going beyond this house.'

Ystayne twitched a smile. 'Oh dear. Do you want to come into town with me later?'

As my phobia was only partly fictional, I said, 'Thanks. I think perhaps I should.'

'Yes, don't let it get too strong a hold.'

There was a pause, then I had to ask. 'Do you know about me, Ystayne?'

He didn't look at me. 'Everyhar knows about you, Gesaril. Gossip flies as quickly here in Kyme as it does anywhere else.'

'What happened in Jesith... It wasn't all my fault, not really.'

He glanced at me again then and grinned. 'Looking at you, lovely, I can see that perfectly.'

'I'm not lovely on the inside.'

Ystayne stood up. 'Who cares? Come to the kitchen after lunch.'

Ystayne, of course, is not your typical Kymian in the Codexia sense. In fact, the community comprises two sorts of hara: the scholars and academics and then everyhar else who looks after them while they wrestle with their mighty thoughts. As I sat on the lawn, it occurred to me that I must eventually be intimate with hara again, and that Ystayne would be more than willing to accommodate me in that regard. Another realisation occurred. I'm more scared of taking aruna than of going out into town. I have no desire for it at all. Physically numb. Ysobi has done this to me. Wretched wretched har. Perhaps if I train myself to hate him, things will be easier for me.

Huriel asked me to join him and Malakess for lunch. There was no way I could eat in front of that har, so I still had to pretend to be ill. After lunch, when Huriel and Malakess had once again retired to Huriel's office for more talk, I went to the kitchen.

'You do look off colour,' Ystayne said. 'Are you sure you want to come out today?'

'Might as well,' I said. 'If I feel weird, can I hold onto your arm?'

'Do so anyway,' Ystayne said. 'I'll enjoy the envious looks it'll earn me.'

And he did get envious looks. We laughed about it. He took me to the market, and I didn't feel strange at all. I wanted to look around some of the old buildings, soak up the atmosphere. Ystayne showed me the black church, which is really bizarre. It's supposed to be a religious building, but it looks like the sort of place where people would have been sacrificed by men wearing cowls. Why would someone build a church out of black bricks? Perhaps they were cheaper. Or maybe the builders really were evil dark magicians. How funny.

We ended our walk by taking tea in a café in the town square. There were trees all around us, the sunlight coming down and flowers growing in old barrels by the café door. Ystayne flirted with me and I half-heartedly responded. He's not a bad-looking har, and quite young, probably second generation like me.

Eventually he asked me: 'Do you sleep alone?'

'Yes, but for the ghosts,' I replied. 'Why?'

'We wonder, Rayzie and me, exactly why Huriel brought you here from Jesith. The answer seems obvious.'

'It's not what you think. He's never touched me.'

Ystayne raised his eyebrows. 'Is the har mad?'

I took a breath. 'I have problems. Huriel knows that. He doesn't desire me, and that's good. I need to be alone for a while, sort my head out.'

Ystayne could not hide his disappointment. 'That's a shame.'

I laughed. 'Don't worry, I'll come knocking on your door the moment I change my mind.'

Ystayne pulled a face. 'Sorry, am I that obvious?'

'Yes.' I reached out and flicked the end of his nose. 'I don't mind.'

'You're used to it, of course.' He shook his head and sighed.

Yes, I am used to it, Ystayne, and to be honest I'm sick of it too. It's like the moment hara see me, they think they have this divine right to possess me. It's as if I have to pay for the fact that I'm beautiful by having to give myself to everyhar who wants me. If I say no, hara think there's something wrong with me, which of course there is. And then, when I do find somehar I really like, this beauty thing gets in the way. He'll think he won't be able to interest me for long, or maybe when he looks at me, he thinks about the thousands of hara I've supposedly taken aruna with, because I'm so irresistible I must be rooning constantly. You see, it's really annoying. Inevitably, I go for those who seem the most challenging

– except perhaps for Huriel. He doesn't have that whiff of danger about him that I like, I think. It's obscene that Malakess looks like Ysobi, because he's a tedious academic and that face doesn't belong to him. Nohar has the right to look like Ysobi and not *be* him. Why can't Huriel *see* it? He could have warned me. Surely he can see it? I'm rambling to myself. Maybe I should shave off my hair and eyebrows. Would that make a difference?

Agavesday, Meadowmoon 28

It's as if the universe has cracked its knuckles and thought *Aha, how can I discomfort this wretched creature even more?* I say this because Malakess has been around a lot the past few weeks. I've become very adept at avoiding him, because every time I see him, I get that cold shock. He is actually a lot more physically attractive than Ysobi, who as I said is rather odd-looking, but to me his looks just seem washed out and pale in comparison, despite the shock I experience each time I lay eyes on him. He gives me strange glances, as if he's just turned over a stone and some weird insect is waving its feelers in his face. No doubt he thinks I'm peculiar. Whenever we bump into each other, which thankfully is only rarely, he'll pause for a moment, then incline his head and say, 'Hello, Gesaril.' It sounds sort of insulting, which should make it easier for me, but it never does.

I've been making friends with Ystayne and Rayzie, who are easy going and, despite claiming to be gossips, never try to question me about the past. Rayzie was the more cautious to begin with, and I thought this might be because he and Ystayne are an item, and Ystayne makes no secret of the fact he likes me, but it isn't that. Rayzie is just cautious with every new har he meets. I'm glad it isn't the same old story, with Rayzie running off to his friends to complain about me being a predator, and so on.

One night, Rayzie and I got drunk together and sat outside in the garden to look at the stars. We sprawled on the lawn that was wet with dew. Once a fox stared at us from the bushes; eyes like topazes. Somewhere nearby, a har was singing; the song came through the evening like a sad memory. I couldn't hear the words, but I didn't need to. It was a song of longing; perhaps it made both Rayzie and I think. He said to me, 'You really are extraordinary to look at, Gesaril. I bet you get fed up with hara lusting after you.'

This was actually the first time anyhar had said this to me, in quite that way. 'I hate it,' I said, tongue loosened by the wine we'd drunk. 'It's like they can't see *me*, and my body is a prison I'm trapped inside.'

Rayzie nodded. 'I can understand that.' He clasped my shoulder. 'Don't worry. It'll get better as you get older.'

'Will it?'

'Yes,' he said. 'You'll have a different kind of beauty then, and because you won't be young anymore, hara won't think they can take liberties or make assumptions. I've noticed myself how hara can be with second generation. It's like we're some kind of delicious treat. They'd never dare treat their peers that way.'

'Did it get better for you?' I asked.

He laughed. 'I'm not in your league, but yes, it did.' He paused. 'Soume is strong in the young. It makes us seem like young women, and a lot of first generation, who of course all used to be men, don't realise that appeals to them so much. They have a tendency to treat us in a similar way to how men used to treat women.'

I'd never heard such an astounding idea, mainly because I'd never thought about it. 'What do you mean? How did men treat women?'

Again, he laughed. 'Like hara treat you! Sweetmeats for the bedroom... sometimes. Women had to fight to get political power. I study anthropology – that's the study of humans - whenever I can, because I used to feel a bit like you do now.'

'Was that why you wanted to be in Kyme, to study?'

He shrugged. 'Partly. It's difficult to get work in the houses of the Codexiae, and Huriel has been good to me.'

'But you clean his home!' I exclaimed. 'Why aren't you studying with him like me?'

'My parents don't have much to barter with, and certainly no coin,' Rayzie said.

'Oh.' I didn't tell him that my education was free, simply to get me away from Jesith and the tarnished reputation of the esteemed Ysobi. 'Do you mind cleaning the house?'

'No,' Rayzie said. 'It's very relaxing and I can think while I'm doing it. Nohar bothers me.'

'I like it here too,' I said. 'In some ways, it seems enchanted, like I've left life behind and have come to live in a dream.'

Rayzie nodded. 'Huriel is a good har. He treats us all like family, but that's because he has none, I suppose.'

'He doesn't have a chesnari,' I said. 'Has he ever had anyhar special?'

'I've been here for three years, and the answer is no, not in my time. Ystayne and I know he has *liaisons*, but he's always discreet about them. He's a strange one. Comes from being a scholarly type, I expect. In human times, they were often anti-social creatures. Hara can't be that different. Huriel loves words more than hara.'

'You seem to know a lot about humans,' I said.

'We should all know,' Rayzie replied. 'Otherwise, we could end up the same way.'

'Does Huriel know about your thoughts?' I couldn't resist asking.

Rayzie twisted his mouth to the side. 'He knows I like studying.'

'Maybe you should talk to him. I don't think income

is his first priority when it comes to education. You should be doing something other than cleaning houses, Rayzie.'

Rayzie shook his head, but he was grinning. My comment had pleased him. 'Perhaps. Like you, I enjoy life here. I'm not eager for change.'

I sensed he wanted me to drop the subject, so I did, but it made me think.

Today was an interesting day, in the sense of interesting being somewhat grotesque and unexpected. At breakfast, Huriel announced he wished for me to help the High Codexia that morning. He did this without looking at me, which should have perhaps told me something.

'What?' I exclaimed. 'Why?'

'He needs somehar to take notes for him, for a report he's sending to Immanion. You're quick at writing things down. I think it'd be good for you.'

'I'd rather not,' I said. 'I'll do anything else. Ask Rayzie to do it. I'm sure he'd like to.'

'*Rayzie?*' Huriel raised his brows, smothered a smile. 'I don't think so, Gesaril. This is part of *your* job.'

'The High Codexia intimidates me.'

'All the more reason to do what I ask. You shouldn't be intimidated. He doesn't judge you as much as you think.'

Since I hadn't even considered Malakess might judge me, this told me he probably did. For some reason, Huriel had set his heart on me becoming acquainted with his mentor. Perhaps he sensed undercurrents of discomfort in the house. Whatever I said, he wouldn't listen to me. I couldn't tell him the real reason for my lack of enthusiasm, though.

So, I had to steel myself for this encounter. I could write fast, and if I kept quiet, Malakess might speak quickly. The whole idea of the High Codexia annoyed me intensely. I couldn't forgive him for his appearance, because I still thought he had no right to look like that.

At least I wouldn't have to go to his house or his office in the library, since he was coming here to Huriel's. He spends a lot of time here. It makes me wonder whether his own house isn't very homely.

When he arrived, Huriel called me from the kitchen, where I was talking with Ystayne and Rayzie. I'd needed inane chatter to keep the monsters in my head at bay. Dutifully, I went to Huriel's office, note pad and pen in hand. It couldn't be that difficult, I kept telling myself, because this is *not* Ysobi. You must remember that.

I closed the door to Huriel's office behind me, sensing the presence of another, even though I didn't raise my eyes. I sat down before the desk, behind which Malakess loomed invisibly, and said, 'I'm ready, tiahaar. Please dictate to me. I can write very fast.'

He dictated to me for over an hour, so that my fingers began to ache. His voice was nothing like Ysobi's sensual low tones, being quite brittle and formal. What he dictated to me was dry, all about the dissemination of knowledge from human times, and how hara needed to be educated to believe it wasn't inherently evil. Rayzie would have been so much more suited for this job. Malakess thought that not everything from the old days was bad, and much of it should be salvaged. I couldn't disagree with that. But he went on to reiterate (to the hara who would read his words and know this fact well, of course) that some tribes have a visceral loathing of anything human, especially their technology and industry. Malakess was trying to propose a middle way, which did not exploit the world or its creatures, but which was forward looking.

After an hour, he paused. 'Stop writing,' he said.

I did so.

Malakess sighed. 'So many hara have said these things before, not least members of the Hegemony in

Immanion. Why should I think I can make a difference?'

I didn't reply, simply because I didn't think he expected me to.

He laughed coldly. 'I take it you agree with me, then.'

'I have no opinion, tiahaar,' I said, 'since I don't have the experience to judge.'

'But what do you *think*, Gesaril? You're second generation. You're not tainted by preconceptions. Tell me what you think.'

I shrugged awkwardly, examining the pen in my hands. 'I don't know. Everything I've heard sounds like a good idea to me, but then I haven't heard any other har talk this way.' I paused. 'Except for my friend, Rayzie, who works here. He's very interested in anthropology.' I was glad I could remember the word.

'Are you interested in it?'

'I like to listen to Rayzie,' I said. 'Is there still anything you wish me to take down, tiahaar?'

There was a silence from behind the desk. I wondered if I'd been too rude. I wished he wouldn't try to talk to me.

Then he said, 'Gesaril.'

I squirmed, but tried not to show it. 'Yes, tiahaar?'

'Will you look at me?'

Reluctantly, I raised my eyes for a second, let them get scorched, then lowered my gaze.

I heard him sigh. 'Look at me, please. For more than a second.'

What choice did I have? I looked up and saw Ysobi sitting there. I tried to think there was no similarity, or that what similarity existed was only small. It was like putting pins into my eyes. 'Yes, tiahaar?'

'I have to say something about this, because it puzzles me. Whenever I run into you, you look at me as if I'm about to torture you to death and then you flee. Have I unwittingly offended you?'

I'm not prone to blushing, but coloured up at that. 'No… no tiahaar. Nothing.'

'Then, why? You haven't looked at me once today since you've been here, until I asked you to. Is this some extravagant form of etiquette you were taught at home?'

I shook my head. 'Not really. I wish only to be polite.'

'It's more than that,' he said. 'I can sense it. I think you should tell me.'

'I would like to go now, please,' I said desperately.

He was silent another moment, during which time I looked away from him, then I heard him say, 'Yes, go.'

I fled.

Later, Huriel came to me. I was sitting on my bed staring at the notes I had written, my heart still staggering and reeling at different moments.

'Would you write out what Malakess dictated to you in a neat hand?' Huriel asked.

I nodded. 'Of course.'

Huriel sat on my bed and folded his arms, always a sign he felt we needed to talk. Now, I couldn't even look at *him*. 'Gesaril,' he said. 'I think we should have a little chat.'

I didn't say anything.

'Malakess isn't pleased,' he said. 'Why are you so rude to him?'

'I'm not,' I said. 'I don't mean to be.'

'You've obviously taken an instant dislike to him, which I find perplexing. He's not a har to dislike, Gesaril.'

'I have no opinion about him,' I said. 'I don't know him.'

Huriel exhaled through his nose. 'I insist that you tell

me what the problem is.'

In those words were the reminders of how much Huriel had given me, with no cost attached, of any kind. I looked at him then. 'It'll sound really stupid. I don't want to tell you.'

He displayed his palms. 'I don't care how stupid it is, I just want to know.'

I took a deep breath. 'I'm surprised you haven't guessed. I can't believe you haven't guessed.'

'Guessed what?' He sounded exasperated.

'Malakess looks like Ysobi,' I said, hating the words, because they really did sound stupid.

Huriel frowned. 'Does he?'

'You must know he does!' I blurted. 'How can you not see it?'

He shrugged. 'Well... I suppose there is a slight resemblance... the hair, the shape.... They are both unusually tall. I don't know. Is this why you've been so rude to him?'

'It's his eyes,' I said, realising it for the first time, those piercing, unsettling cobalt eyes, 'and yes, the hair, the shape.'

'Hmmm,' murmured Huriel. 'In that case, you should probably confront the problem. There's no sense in trying to avoid him. It's ridiculous. He's not Ysobi, you know that. Do you desire him?'

'No!' How could Huriel think that? Rayzie would say it's because he's first generation.

Huriel shifted on the bed. 'Well, seeing as Malakess is my closest friend as well as my mentor, he deserves an explanation. You must tell him. He's concerned he's affronted you in some way.'

'You tell him!' I said 'Really, it's nothing. I know it's ridiculous. Please... no... don't tell him. I'll work with him tomorrow and the day after. I'll look at him and be nice. I promise.'

'No, Gesaril.' Huriel was stern. 'You went through a harrowing experience in Jesith. This is part of the healing process. You must tell Malakess your thoughts. Look him in the face and realise he's nothing like Ysobi at all. This is for you, not for him.'

'I can't believe you'd put me through that,' I said bitterly.

'It's because I care for you that I can,' he said gently. 'Really, Gesaril, Malakess is no ghost. He's different. You need to see that.'

'I love him... Ysobi,' I said.

Huriel nodded once. 'I know.' He paused. 'If you wish to speak to me about it, you can, you know. I know Ysobi very well.'

'Then why should you want to listen to me?'

Huriel gave me a gentle smile. I wanted to trust him. 'I know you're not a fool. And it's sometimes better to get something out in the open rather than keep it locked up inside... don't you think?'

I nodded. 'I really want to hate him, but I can't. Why is that? When I see his face in my head, I think he's not even that attractive.' I put my head in my hands, rubbed my temples hard. 'Why did he affect me so, Huriel? Why can't I banish him from my head and my heart? It makes no sense. He abandoned me to the wolves. That's what it felt like. He made me love him, then he threw me away. How can I love a har like that?'

I glanced at Huriel and he was inspecting me keenly. I realised I'd said something that had either surprised or angered him. 'What do you mean exactly?' he asked crisply.

'You know,' I said. 'You know the story.'

'I know that you demanded something from him emotionally, then caused trouble when your... desire...

38

wasn't reciprocated. Ysobi has a certain effect on hara, especially given the nature of his work. I don't think he realised what he was doing to you, and in that way I can see you weren't totally responsible.'

I couldn't help but laugh. 'Who told you all that? Him?'

'Perhaps I would like to hear your side of it now.'

'What is there to say? He said so many things to me, and if he didn't mean them, it makes him a monster. I thought... I was given to believe my feelings were returned. Do you think I would have abased myself like that otherwise? I do have pride, you know.'

Huriel put his head to one side, stared at me, and I wouldn't flinch away from his gaze. 'Looking at you, I can see you are telling the truth as you see it.'

'As I see it?' I thumped the bed with both hands. 'It was unmistakeable, even though since then I've sometimes questioned my own sanity about it. I wish I could replay my memories for you, like pictures on a wall. That is the cruelty of it all, doubting myself. Do you understand?'

'Tell me everything,' he said. 'I want to know.'

And so I did; all the trivial little details I could remember. The conversations we'd had, when I'd known, in the deepest core of my heart, the subject under discussion was not always what it appeared to be. The hidden language of love; a love so secret, so forbidden, it had be disguised in pictures, in code. Aruna had been part of my training, yes, but in fact Ysobi and I had been more intimate in other ways. The glances that had lingered too long. The knowledge in a har's eyes. The way my flesh had ignited when he'd stood behind me and the aura of his body had touched mine. His voice. His gaze holding mine. He had stared into my eyes and said these things. *I will always be here. I'm not*

*going anywhere. You can say anything to me...
anything. We must be honest with each other.*

He had taken my hands in his. He had held me for
hours as I'd spilled my heart to him. *I'm not who you
think I am. I'm not worth it.* But still he'd held me, and
still we had continued along that treacherous path we'd
set our feet upon.

Black crows in a white sky, flying away. His words.

As I relived this pain, so vivid because in my mind it
wasn't a memory, it was still happening, I tried to speak
as honestly as I could. I tried to be objective. That's
difficult when you're trying to convince somehar you're
not mad or a liar. Even as I was speaking, a mean little
voice inside me was saying, 'ah, but did it really happen
that way?' I spoke so openly, I forgot who I was
speaking to. I wonder if that was a mistake?

When I ran out of words, Huriel stood up and walked
to the window. He stared out of it for some moments,
then shook his head. 'I don't know what to say. That is a
very different account to what I've been told.'

'Of course it is. But do you believe me?'

He came back to me. 'How can I not when you
speak with such rawness? How can I not believe you
when I look into your eyes and see your pain? It's my
belief no har can feel as you do and it not be based
upon... *something.*' He grimaced. 'Ysobi was one of my
most gifted students, and sometimes he scared me with
his intensity. Hara are drawn to him, and although he
might like to be modest about it, I think he knows only
too well what effect he can have, and it's my belief he
uses that for his own advantage, consciously or not. He
likes to be liked, to be loved.' Huriel sighed, and for a
brief moment looked wistful.

I stared at him, shocked, wondering whether Ysobi
had exercised his arunic arts on this dry, bookish har.

40

Huriel laughed, clearly having picked up my loud, unguarded thoughts. 'It was part of our training, Gesaril, although perhaps not as great a part as you experienced.' He patted my shoulder. 'Whatever happened, it's done. If he broke your heart, then let it mend. Don't bring Ysobi here with you. Make your life anew. Part of that is banishing the phantoms. You do understand me, don't you?'

I inclined my head. 'Yes. I understand.'

'I've told Malakess what a bright har you are. He knows how highly I regard you. It would please me if you could be comfortable in his presence.'

I can see the sense in it. Ysobi has no right to be here, nor to possess Malakess in my eyes.

Later

I walked through a miserable drizzle to the house of Malakess. It was actually a lot smaller than Huriel's and nowhere near as interesting. I really can't say what was on my mind as I trudged up the drive. I wasn't as nervous or angry as I could have been. Neither did I fear humiliation. It was strange. I told myself the old Gesaril would have made a big drama out of this situation; the new Gesaril would sort out the problem quickly so he didn't have to brood about it.

The front door to the house was weathered and the brass knocker, in the shape of a lion's head, was dull with neglect. An ancient wisteria grew up the side of the house, but it needed pruning and tidying, since it had lots of dead branches within it, and the living bits covered many of the windows. It seemed I'd been right about Malakess's abode; no wonder he preferred the comforts of Huriel's house. I banged the knocker three times and imagined the sound reverberating through empty corridors. Would Malakess have furniture? Maybe he only lived in a couple of rooms.

After only a short wait the door opened. I'd prepared my speech, but then found myself tongue-tied, because it wasn't Malakess who'd answered my knock. I should have anticipated he'd have staff. After all, he was High Codexia. A young har stood before me, refined of feature with long fairish hair. He peered at me in enquiry, which suggested this household didn't receive many visitors.

'Good day, tiahaar,' I began. 'Is Tiahaar Malakess at home?'

The har before me frowned a little. 'He's very busy. I'm his assistant. Can I take a message?'

Oh, so he was a guard dog. I inclined my head. 'Not really. I work for Tiahaar Huriel, and he has asked me to speak to Tiahaar Malakess personally.'

The har wasn't convinced, I could tell, but he thought about it for a few seconds, then relented. 'You'd better come in.'

I too bowed my head politely and stepped over the threshold. Inside, I could smell roses and the hallway was surprisingly light and airy. A white tiled floor supported a well polished table and a stand by the door for coats. Perhaps Malakess was renovating this house gradually.

'Wait here,' said the assistant and marched off down a corridor straight ahead. He had the same proprietorial air that Jassenah in Jesith had had; maybe Malakess was his Ysobi. Suddenly, the idea of my confession became infinitely less attractive.

I didn't have to wait long. After only a minute or so, the assistant returned. His expression was not at all friendly. 'He'll see you. Follow me.'

I said nothing, but complied with his order. He led me into the house and paused at a door, upon which he knocked with a single knuckle. It all seemed a bit ridiculous to me, since Malakess knew I was here. A voice came from the room within: 'Enter!'

The assistant opened the door, pulled a mordant face at me, and indicated I should obey the words of the great har. 'Thank you,' I said, smiling sweetly, and stepped into the room. The door was closed behind me so swiftly, the resulting gust of wind nearly made me stagger.

This was clearly Malakess's office. There were book shelves, but they weren't as crammed as Huriel's were. The desk was also smaller and suspiciously tidy. I got the impression that Malakess had come here swiftly to meet me, and that the room wasn't used much usually. He was leaning against the desk, arms folded, a tall lean shape poured perfectly into the room. His hands were amazing. 'What can I do for you, Gesaril?' he asked. 'Huriel has a message for me?'

'Not exactly,' I replied. 'He suggested I come and speak to you.' This was not going to be easy, I could tell. Perhaps I should make an excuse and leave.

Malakess nodded once. 'Sit down... please.' He moved behind the desk and took a seat there. Now this was like a formal interview.

I sat down on a window seat, which was in fact the only available place, and it was just a fraction too far from the desk for comfort. I might even have to raise my voice a little. This was absurd. 'Huriel thinks I've been disrespectful to you,' I said, improvising my script wildly, since I now realised I hadn't a clue what to say.

Malakess raised his eyebrows. 'And you're here to apologise?'

'Yes... I'm sorry.' There, that had been surprisingly easy.

'So, are you going to tell me now the reason behind your behaviour?'

Hmm, I wasn't going to get away that easily after all. I refused to squirm, but steeled myself to look him in the eye. It was like being struck by a small bolt of lightning; those same electric eyes. A small cold part of me suspected Malakess knew exactly what I felt, but was cruel enough to make me say it. I wouldn't give him the satisfaction of seeing me suffer. 'It has never been rudeness, but discomfort,' I said, trying to sound aloof and objective. 'You remind me of somehar, that's all. Sometimes, it's difficult to ignore the jolts of recognition a deceptively familiar face invokes. There's nothing more to it than that. I never intended to offend you, tiahaar.'

'Who do I remind you of?'

I still held his gaze. He thought this was very amusing. 'I think you know,' I said, hopefully with dignity, and got to my feet. Whatever Huriel's fond projections for this meeting, it was clear they would never be realised.

'Oh, do sit down, Gesaril,' Malakess said, laughing. 'I'm sorry. I don't know, actually. I just hope it was somehar presentable.'

I wouldn't sit down again, but decided not to leave just yet. 'You know my history?' I asked.

Malakess displayed his palms, shrugged. 'Some of it. You came from Jesith under a cloud. You're reputed to be a troublesome young thing, or maybe just troubled. It's not my concern. It's the past. Why dwell on it?'

'I trained in Jesith under Ysobi. You know of him?'

Malakess nodded, pulled down the corners of his mouth in rather a caustic smile. 'Of course,' he said dryly. 'One of Kyme's brightest students, a credit to our academy.'

'Our relationship became... unprofessional,' I said. 'It caused problems in the community. I had to leave.'

Malakess frowned. 'I'm not sure I understand you, but then I don't really want to know. What has this to do with me?'

'You look like him. You look like Ysobi.' There, it was said. I braced myself for his response.

'Oh... A bad reminder. I see.' He smiled more naturally. 'Do I really look like him? I can't see it myself.'

'It seems I'm the only one who can.'

'So you're afraid I'll be harsh with you? You're expecting criticism or punishment, maybe? Please don't think that. I know nothing about you, really. I don't care what you did in Jesith. As long as you work well here, that's all that matters. And from what I've heard, you're doing very well.'

In those words, I sensed an impending dismissal. He didn't get it at all: thank the dehara. 'Well... thank you,' I said, ducking my head. 'I won't keep you any longer. It was important to Huriel I explain myself to you, and I intend to put all the ghosts behind me. I appreciate you listening to me. I must sound very stupid.'

Malakess waved a hand at me. 'Think nothing of it. I appreciate your honesty also. I can see you find this difficult.'

I nodded. 'I'm glad I came. Huriel was right.'

I began to walk towards the door but Malakess called me back. 'Gesaril, please sit down again. I'd like to know more about you, your aspirations and so on. Has Huriel devised a programme of work for you? What about your caste training? Would you like tea? And don't sit over there. You'll find a chair outside the door in the hallway. Bring that in, sit by me.'

One thing I think I learned about Malakess that day was that he is not naturally devious, nor prone to playing subtle mind games. I told him I wasn't sure what I wanted for the future, but that I enjoyed my work with Huriel, and that eventually I'd know what I wanted to do with my life.

'True, you have plenty of time,' Malakess said. 'You could train to become a codexia or a hienama here, if you wish.' He waved an arm to indicate the entire room. 'Look at this place. Nearly everything in this house is old, and was built or devised by humans. What will happen when it all wears out? Wraeththu need hara with fine minds for the future. There is much we have to accomplish.'

'I know what you mean,' I said, warming to the subject, since it was something I'd often discussed with

Rayzie. 'For example, every house has a clock, but do we have enough skilled clockmakers to repair them or make new ones?' I shrugged. 'Clocks are just one thing.'

'Quite,' said Malakess. 'We want clocks but we don't want factories or intensive industry, but maybe there are some who do.' He tapped his lips with the fingers of one hand, staring out of the window. 'What we have to decide is what is valid and useful, what luxuries are reasonable, and how to manufacture things without causing pollution or waste.'

'It's a very big task,' I said.

'That's why I work with the Gelaming,' Malakess said. 'They have their faults, but also their uses.'

'Hmm...'

'You should go to Immanion one day. You'd find it interesting.' He put his head to one side. 'Where do you come from?'

'The Shadowvales, not far from Jesith. Our community is an example of all that is best and worst about the Sulh.'

Malakess laughed. 'I have heard of it. I wouldn't have said worst... why do you say that?'

I shrugged awkwardly. 'Hara there don't live in reality. They think the world is a benevolent place, and when things don't conform to that idea, they ignore them.'

'Perhaps they are simply trying to create a better reality by living it.'

I laughed harshly. 'Perhaps.' That pathetic ideal had ruined my life. I wasn't allowed to have horrors in my past. They had been ignored, pushed away, so that they condensed deep inside me only to leak out like poison.

There was a silence, and I didn't even notice it. Malakess broke it, softly. 'What happened to you, Gesaril?'

I debated whether to tell him. I'd kept silent in Jesith until it had been too late. 'When I was a young harling, some friends and I were attacked by rogue hara. My parents…' I shook my head. 'They didn't know how to deal with it, so they thought it best to ignore it.'

'Were they ever caught, the attackers?' Malakess asked sharply.

'No. They were long gone by the time I managed to get home. I was lucky to survive. Others were taken, one killed.'

'I'm… I'm very sorry to hear that,' Malakess said. He paused. 'Does Huriel know of this?'

'Not yet,' I said, sure that Malakess would tell him.

'Did you suffer any… lasting injuries?'

'Yes,' I said. 'I think so. But more of the mind than the body.'

'Understandable,' Malakess said. 'Perfectly so. Is this what caused your problem in Jesith?'

'Yes and no… it was complicated.'

'Do you want to talk about it?'

'You said you didn't want to know.'

'It's different now.'

I sighed. 'No, I don't want to talk about it. Thank you, but no.' The only har I'd ever talked to about it, apart from Huriel, was Jassenah, of all hara; Ysobi's chesnari. I'd thought him my worst enemy, but he'd saved me in Jesith. Without him, I'd be dead. He'd chased my phantoms away, the ones I'd dragged with me for many years. He'd chased them away once Ysobi had abandoned me to myself. It is hard to hate Jassenah now.

'Take care with yourself,' Malakess said gently. 'Don't keep things inside that need to come out. I don't wish to sound patronising, but I am an ancient being in comparison to you, and believe me I saw and experienced many hideous things in the early days.'

I nodded. 'I appreciate that.'

'You know,' Malakess said, 'us incepted hara are completely aware of what the pure born think of us. But one thing you should consider: we at least have the experience of what it's like to be afraid, what it's like to suffer pain and cruelty, to live on the run, with no sanctuary, surrounded by those who can't be trusted. Sometimes, in some situations, we are the best hara to speak to. Do you understand me?'

'Utterly,' I said. 'Thank you.' I wondered then what had happened to him, once long ago.

So despite my early misgivings, Huriel had in fact been right. Malakess was a decent and wise har, and I'd ended up enjoying his company. The more we'd talked, the less he'd discomforted me. Ysobi will fade from him slowly; it's an exorcism.

When I finally left Malakess's house, even the sky had cleared. I felt surprisingly light of spirit and decided to wander into town for a while. All around me, hara were going about their daily business. I felt invisible among them. My feet led me to the markets and there I browsed among the stalls. I walked down an aisle where everyhar sold curios, human artefacts scavenged from the ruins of long dead towns. Beyond this were merchants selling herbs and sachets, and equipment for the occult arts. I paused to peruse the wares of a young har who carved beautiful little boxes from various types of wood.

'Every one of them is different,' he told me.

I nodded and picked up one of the smallest boxes. *This is the one*, I thought. 'How much?' I asked the vendor.

'Three bits to you,' he replied. It was ridiculously cheap.

I smiled charmingly. 'Thank you.' I nodded towards a treasure heap of crystals that were strewn upon a cloth of black velvet on the stall. 'I'll take a quartz also.'

'You can have one for free,' said the har. He grinned. 'Don't take advantage. At least pick a small one.'

I laughed and did so. It didn't matter how big the stone was; this was only a gesture. 'Can you wrap it in something for me?'

The har nodded. 'It's a gift, then?'

'Yes. Yes it is.'

I watched the har's nimble brown fingers wrap up my purchase in what appeared to be handmade paper dyed blue. He bound it with twine and handed it to me. 'Some har is lucky to be receiving a present from you,' he said.

'No, it is me who is lucky,' I replied and gave him the money. 'Thank you.'

After this, I went to a café and ordered a mug of the locally brewed cider. I asked the proprietor if he had writing implements, and he gave me a pen and some ink. I sat outside in the garden at the back of the café and wrote upon my parcel: Jassenah har Jesith, Lyonis. I hoped I had just enough money left to send it to him.

The mail bureau wasn't very busy that day. I asked how long it would take for the package to reach Jesith and the clerk replied, 'A despatch to the south goes out in two days. Given the route, it can take up to a month for items to reach their destination, but it's often sooner than that. Depends what the rider has to deliver and where.'

I was pleased to discover that quite a lot of mail was scheduled for the south; this meant that the clerk was happy to charge me a pittance for my small delivery. 'There's a pile going to Jesith,' he said. 'As you must know, quite a lot of communication passes between here and there.'

I hadn't known that, but looked upon it as a fortunate circumstance.

I had considered whether I should write a letter to Jassenah, but somehow I couldn't find the heart to do it. I'd considered sending the package anonymously, but then on impulse, before I finally handed it over to the mail clerk, I asked for a pen and wrote 'from Gesaril, Kyme' on the back. I hoped the gesture of the exquisite little box and its pure sparkling contents would imply what I wanted it to imply.

Huriel was pleased with me, and didn't question why I'd been out for most of the day. Perhaps he thought I'd spent all that time with Malakess. As the afternoon faded into evening, I began to feel uncomfortable about the package I'd sent to Jassenah. Was I sending it to him merely to maintain some kind of contact, no matter how tenuous, with Ysobi? My mind said not, but I wasn't sure it could be trusted. I even considered going to the mail bureau in the morning to retrieve the package. But in the end I decided to let it go. I would deliver it into the hands of fate. Jassenah might throw my gift into the nearest pond, for all I knew.

Pelfazzarsday, Ardourmoon 8

An invitation has come. How could he? I can't write any more today.

So, this is what happened yesterday…

A function was being held at the Academy, in honour of a visiting delegation of Nagini, hara from a hot country far to the east. Malakess was invited to this party, naturally, and had sent me an invitation asking if I'd accompany him. Clearly, Huriel expected me to react with surprise and pleasure to the invitation, but honestly I felt sick and disappointed. I'd believed Malakess had understood and respected me; he'd seemed like the impartial teacher that Ysobi had never been. But then this. While Huriel enthused about what a privilege this was for me, I sat there in silence, staring at the note, thinking differently. All the time while we'd been speaking, Malakess had been like any other har and had wanted me. That's what this was all about. As if he cared about whether or not I met dignitaries from a foreign land. He wanted me on his arm, no doubt, to show off to his colleagues, and then later he'd expect me to swoon into his bed. It was tiresomely predictable.

'What's the matter?' Huriel asked, his excitement punctured by the fact I wasn't sharing it.

I shrugged. 'Well… I just didn't expect this.'

'It's an amazing opportunity,' Huriel said. 'Not just anyhar gets invited to Academy functions, you know. I haven't been asked to this one! And the hara from the Nagini are extremely high-ranking. Imagine what tales they'll have to tell. We know so little of what goes on in other lands.'

'*I* haven't been invited,' I said. 'Malakess just had an invite for himself and a companion.'

'So what?' Huriel paused and frowned. 'I thought everything was fine between you and Kess now.'

'It is... well I thought it was. Why does he want me to go, Huriel?'

'It's simply a generous gesture,' Huriel replied. 'What do you mean?'

I sighed. 'He could have asked me back to his house to teach me. He could have offered me work. He could even have told me about this event while I was with him.' I shook my head. 'No, he's been thinking about me, that's all. I'm sure he's telling himself he's concerned for me, and can help me, but ultimately it's just down to the same old thing.'

Huriel's expression had become flinty. 'If you're referring to intimacy, then surely that's an intrinsic part of our being? If, indeed, he does wish to know you better, how can that possibly offend you?'

I pressed my hands briefly against my eyes. 'I don't know,' I said, 'but it does. It's the assumption, maybe...'

Huriel expressed a humourless laugh. 'Gesaril, you're a lovely har, you and I both know that. Perhaps Malakess does desire you. Wouldn't you be more offended if he didn't?'

I glanced at him; he was regarding me with his head to one side. 'No, I wouldn't. You don't understand.'

'The way I see it, if one har desires another, he initiates some kind of social event in order to find out whether anything else is viable. Perhaps that *is* what your invitation's about, but perhaps not. In either case, you should just go and enjoy yourself. You're under no obligation to do anything you don't want to do.'

'I don't want anything embarrassing to happen.'

Huriel rolled his eyes. 'Oh, for the Ag's sake, what kind of har do you think Malakess is? He can read signals, you know. Just go, Gesaril. Stop fretting about everything. If you don't want to be with Malakess, fine, but there might be other hara there you like. One day you're going to have to crawl out of that den you've built for yourself. You can't remain alone for ever. It's bad for you.'

'I suppose so.'

'I *know* so! Also, it will do you good to dress up and revel in your own loveliness for an evening. You never pay attention to how you look, and I can tell that's not really in your nature.'

'I haven't got any suitable clothes, nothing formal, anyway.'

'I'll get you something.'

'Huriel, no! You've done enough for me as it is.' I don't know why I bothered protesting, since it was obvious Huriel had already made up his mind.

And so, at my friend and mentor's injunction, I have asked Ystayne to drop a note over to Malakess's house saying that I am grateful for the invite and yes, I'd be delighted to accompany him to the Academy party. It has occurred to me that Malakess's assistant should be the har to stand at his side at this important function. A wing of foreboding brushes my heart. How will this har feel when he finds out about my role in the proceedings? I can't think about that. I've done nothing wrong. I don't even desire Malakess. If hara want to make something more of it, then they can. I don't care.

Arahanisday, Ardourmoon 20

I feel as if I'm about to go through feybraiha again, or take a blood bond, or something. The household has been thrown into a flurry of the vapours at the prospect of my night out. Huriel ordered an assortment of clothes for me from Yorvik, Ystayne took me to the brother of a friend of his who trimmed my hair, (it was badly in need of attention, to be honest), while Rayzie insisted on spending nearly a whole day at the monthly fair with me, to buy bits of jewellery to go with my new clothes. I only need one set for the evening; it's insane. It's not as if I'll be able to run off to the bathroom every half hour to change my costume. But Huriel seems to think that the function will open up an entire diary of social events for me, and that I'll need a wardrobe for it. However, despite my initial exasperation, my friends' behaviour is infectious and I'm starting to feel excited and nervous too. It *is* a big thing, far bigger than I'd thought. Phyle leaders from all over Alba Sulh will be at the event, as well as hara from Immanion and other tribes in Almagabra and surrounding countries.

Malakess has been conspicuously absent from the house for the past couple of weeks. At first, I thought this was to do with me, but Huriel told me it was because he's immersed in arrangements for the event, as well as entertaining foreign hara who have already arrived in Kyme. Sometimes we see them in town; imposing hara in unusual clothes. Nohar has seen the Nagini yet, although they were supposed to have arrived two days ago. The party takes place tomorrow. This time tomorrow I will be getting ready for it.

Pelfazzarsday, Ardourmoon 21

I have tried on all my clothes at least three times each, standing before my mirror, eyeing myself critically. I've managed to persuade everyhar else in the house to leave me alone for an hour. This has displeased them greatly, and I feel a bit mean, because I know they want to share at least a small part of my big night out. But I need to be alone. I need to be with myself, the self who's been curled up in my heart these past few months. Also, I think conflicting opinions about what I should wear would be confusing. I've eventually opted for a pair of wide loose trousers in dark forest green silk velvet, with a plain black silk top and an embroidered thigh length jacket that matches the trousers. I've never worn such costly garments before. It does wonders for the self esteem. My reflection doesn't look like me. I've kept the accessories understated and haven't done anything too shocking with my hair, despite the collection of jewelled pins, carved spikes and so on that Rayzie found for me. I've only brushed it and left it loose. It just touches my shoulders again, now that it's been cut, and looks thicker. As for cosmetics, I'm still vain enough to think I don't need them. I've simply applied the lightest brush of kohl around my eyes. When I'd finished my preparations, I took one last look at myself in the glass. Well, this is it. I'm about to walk out of my safe hiding place into the social world of Kyme. I have no idea where it will lead, but at least I feel excited about it.

Well, a lot happened last night; some good, some not so good. I think I've made a complete fool of myself – again.

Once I'd finished getting ready, I went down to Huriel and the others, who were waiting in the sitting room for me. I made a grand entrance, as they expected me to do. Pausing at the threshold, I struck a pose and said, 'Well, here I am. Will I do?'

Ystayne laughed loudly, Rayzie grinned and rolled his eyes, and Huriel said, 'I think you know the answer to that! Here, have a glass of wine before Kess's carriage arrives. Nervous?'

I went to take the glass off him and sat down on the edge of the sofa. 'Yes. Very. I hope I don't say anything stupid to the wrong har.'

'Just stick by Malakess,' Huriel said. 'He won't abandon you.'

I drank some wine. 'He'd better not!'

Within minutes we heard the sound of horses' hooves upon the gravel outside the house. A hot wave coursed through me. This was it. I stood up and handed my empty glass to Huriel. He hugged me and kissed my cheek. 'You look marvellous,' he said softly. 'Rejoice in yourself, my dear. This is your time.'

I kissed him briefly on the lips. 'Thanks, Huriel, for everything.'

He squeezed me. 'Go. Don't keep him waiting.'

While my new family stood in the window bay to watch me leave, I went into the hallway alone. I faced the great front door, took a breath, and opened it. Two black horses stood stamping on the drive, harnessed to an elegant black carriage. The driver touched his brow, in a gesture of greeting and appreciation. I inclined my head. Malakess opened the carriage door for me and I went to him.

The Academy of Kyme lies a couple of miles outside the town, so I had plenty of time to get more anxious and nervous than I already was. Malakess complimented me on my appearance and then made small talk, most of which I didn't even hear. He was dressed all in black, his long dark red hair loose upon his breast, but for a couple of thin braids on each side. He was wearing kohl too, which made him look very different. His fingers were crammed with glittering rings and I could tell the stones were real gems, not glass. Like me, Malakess had put on for the evening a costume that was more than clothes. Tonight, he was High Codexia and must maintain an image.

When we were close to the Academy, Malakess leaned forward in his seat towards me. 'Be wary of any Gelaming,' he said. 'They will descend upon you like hawks, and before you know it... well, anything could happen. You could wake up in a bed in Immanion.'

'I hope you'll protect me,' I said, rather tersely.

Malakess smiled. 'I'll do my best, but we're bound to get distracted and separated at times. Try to stay close. I'll be swamped, but I'll keep an eye out for you. Use this night to your advantage, Gesaril. Be alert for any opportunities.'

'Such as Gelaming beds?'

'Only if that is your preference.'

I grimaced. 'No. Beds of any kind are not my preference at the moment.'

He said nothing to that, and the silence was slightly

uncomfortable. Before I could stop myself, my mouth had blurted, 'Why did you ask me to come with you?'

He gazed at me steadily, and for a moment that old ghost swarmed over him. I looked away. 'Honestly? I am High Codexia. I want the most beautiful har in Kyme to be next to me tonight. You will be my protection too.'

I wasn't quite sure what he meant by that.

Every window in the Academy was aflame, it seemed. It is a huge building, hundreds of years old, and was once a stately home. Now it was a college, a local government centre, and a temporary home for important hara who came visiting from afar.

Carriages clustered in the driveway, guests milled around, while stable hara ran around trying to organise the parking of the vehicles. It was utter chaos. We couldn't get the carriage anywhere near the main entrance, so the driver dropped us off halfway down the drive. Malakess and I walked together in silence, some feet apart, until the light from the great building fell over us. Then he took one of my hands and hooked it through his elbow. The show had begun.

'This night is very important to you, isn't it?' I said.

Malakess nodded. 'Yes. We want Kyme to be the repository for all Wraeththu knowledge. We want the Hegemony of Immanion to endorse us officially. We want students from other lands, and support to encourage the arts and learning, both here and afar. The Gelaming consider themselves the only ones capable of, or suitable for, such a task. They want Immanion to be the centre of everything. I have to convince them it's in their interests to share control.'

'Shouldn't you have been here at the beginning?' I asked. 'You know, when everyhar arrived?'

He laughed softly. 'Oh, I have my staff for that. I

decided to arrive later. Don't want to appear too eager or desperate.'

'Your assistant will be there?'

'You mean, Iscane? Yes. He's in charge. Having a wonderful time issuing orders to the rest of the staff, no doubt.'

Well, that answered one question I'd pondered: whether this Iscane would resent me taking his place. He had a more important place, or so it seemed.

Some hara in the driveway recognised Malakess as we strolled up the wide front steps. They bowed and uttered greetings. I was conscious of many curious eyes upon me. Not many high ranking hara in Kyme had seen me before, even if they'd heard of me. They would be wondering who I was and where Malakess had found me. For the first time in months, I felt a flicker of sensuality within me. I wanted to be admired. It amused me to think all these hara would assume I shared Malakess's bed. He was held in such high esteem I couldn't help but feel good about being seen with him. I could never have accompanied Ysobi anywhere in public. I had been his secret, kept hidden away. Jassenah hadn't known everything.

Furious with myself, I dismissed these thoughts. As Huriel said, this was my time. The past no longer mattered. I lifted my head. Jassenah would never attend an event like this.

In the hallway, Iscane was clearly in control of the proceedings. He stood at the door, greeting everyhar who arrived, and then announcing who they were in a loud, ringing voice. When it came to us, he raked me with an icy stare. 'Who is your companion, tiahaar?' he asked Malakess, keeping his cold eyes on me.

'Gesaril har Shadowvales,' Malakess replied.

Iscane announced us and we swept into the entrance

hall. Hara in violet and red livery, dispensing drinks and exquisite morsels of food, mingled with the guests. The lighting was subdued and perfumed oil smoked in glass burners, filling the air with an herbal scent. The marble tiled floor beneath our feet was scattered with red petals. Everyhar present seemed at least two feet taller than me and oozed charisma and power. My hand had become sweaty against Malakess's elegant sleeve. Perhaps for this reason, he disengaged me. 'Would you like a drink?' he asked.

I realised it would not be a good idea to get drunk and perhaps disgrace myself, but thought one or two would do no harm. 'Please.'

Before Malakess could move the two or three steps to the nearest member of staff, a har swooped down upon him and took him by the arm. 'Kess! I thought you'd chosen to ignore your own party. Where have you been?' This har was radiant, confident and – well, what other word can I use? – luscious. He was dressed in a long robe of pale silvery grey fabric, his soft brown hair wound about the kind of fabulous tines that Rayzie had wanted me to wear. I wouldn't have got away with it.

'Chrysm, how nice,' Malakess said mildly and kissed the har's cheek. 'I'm so pleased you were able to come.'

'My pleasure,' the har called Chrysm replied. 'I was intrigued, to be honest. Also, I needed a break from Immanion. You know how it is.'

Malakess inclined his head. 'Of course. You must stay for a couple of days if you can. My house is open to you.'

I didn't think that Malakess's house was really fit for a har of this stature, but I supposed Malakess didn't think he'd accept the invitation anyway.

'We'll see,' Chrysm said. He looked at me for the first time. 'Well! Have you been stealing Gelaming harlings, Kess?'

'No,' Malakess replied. 'This is Gesaril har Shadowvales, Sulh born and bred.' He indicated the har before us. 'Gesaril, this is Tiahaar Chrysm Luel, Hegemon for the Arts, from Immanion.'

I bowed my head. 'Pleased to meet you, tiahaar.' My first Gelaming. I could appreciate what Malakess meant about them.

Chrysm glanced about himself. 'This is an impressive gathering, Kess. Be assured, I am impressed. I hear delegates from the Nagini are here.'

'That is true,' Malakess said.

'How did you manage it? They've rejected all our overtures.'

Malakess left his mind open to me, and it was difficult not to smile. The Nagini wouldn't have anything to do with the Gelaming simply because the Almagabrans assumed they were the cream of Wraeththu. The Nagini considered themselves to be equally creamy, if not more so. 'They are a proud and self contained tribe,' Malakess said. 'One of our ether readers was fortunate enough to make contact with one of their hara one evening, and initiated a careful friendship over the ethers. We invited them here because we respect their knowledge and culture. We thought they would like to see our library.'

'If the Nagini are staying here for some time, I might well take you up on your offer,' Chrysm said.

I sent a quick mind touch to Malakess. *Make him stay at Huriel's.* It was somewhat importunate, I know, but I just did it instinctively. A warm tickle of amusement touched my mind. Malakess understood me perfectly.

'Where are you staying?' he asked the Gelaming.

'In a quaint hotel in town,' Chrysm replied. By quaint, I supposed he meant beneath his standards.

'Perhaps Tiahaar Huriel's manse might be more to

your liking,' Malakess said. 'It's said he has the best house in Kyme.'

'Is he here tonight?'

'No, but Gesaril is part of his household.'

Chrysm laughed. 'Oh? I thought he was part of yours, or do you share?'

I was shocked by that remark; it was incredibly rude, I thought, and just another example of how first generation regarded us young pure borns.

Malakess didn't respond to it. 'Do you want a drink, Chrysm? I was just about to get one for Gesaril and myself.'

'Thanks,' Chrysm said. 'The red wine please. I tried the white and it's disgusting.'

With horror, I watched Malakess move away. What on earth could I say to this thing in front of me?

'I was joking,' Chrysm said.

'Excuse me?'

'About the sharing. That sounded awful. Forgive me. My mouth runs away with me sometimes and my sense of humour is often questionable.'

'Oh... that's all right,' I said. I warmed to him slightly. I suffer from the same trait, after all.

'So, are you studying here in Kyme?'

I was pleased and relieved the Hegemon thought a morsel like me could be here for such a purpose. 'Yes. I'm working with tiahaar Huriel. I live in his house.'

'Have you ever been to Immanion?'

'No. This is the first time I've left Lyonis, where I was born.'

Chrysm clasped one of my shoulders. 'We must remedy that. The next time Malakess comes to Almagabra he must bring you with him. I can tell you'd go down extremely well in Immanion society. You could be Gelaming yourself. I really thought so when I first saw you.'

'Umm, thanks.' I presumed that was a compliment.

Malakess returned with the drinks. 'Shall we move into the main salon, tiahaara?'

'Yes,' Chrysm said, sniffing the glass Malakess had given him. 'I'm here with a few others. Nohar stellar, but some interesting types – a couple of artists and writers. I'll introduce you.'

In the grand salon, a group of musicians were playing softly. High ranking academy staff were recognisable because they were dressed in robes of office; indigo fabric embroidered with silver thread. I didn't think many second generation were present and felt somewhat out of place. I was glad few hara spoke to me.

Chrysm led us over to an alcove where most of his company were conversing together. Gelaming writers and artists are pretty much like what you'd imagine – quite full of themselves, self-appointed geniuses. One of the artists was named Sabarah. He was dressed in exquisitely draped white robes and his hair was almost the same colour, although his eyes were dark. His fingernails were long and unattractively pointed and dug into me when he took hold of my arm to drag me away from our companions. 'I have to paint you,' he announced, as if this was the greatest favour the dehara could bestow.

'Okay,' I responded warily.

'At once. Tomorrow. You have inspired me. I must capture you, before you flit away.'

I sucked my upper lip, at a loss for words. 'Mmm.'

'I am utterly serious,' said Sabarah, eyeing me beadily.

'I'll sit for you, if you would like me to,' I said, wondering if that was what Malakess would want me to do.

'I'll make preliminary sketches. I can return any time to complete the work, or I could have you brought to Immanion.'

I smiled. 'Tiahaar, I regret I would not have the time for such a journey.'

Sabarah raised his eyebrows. 'What do you mean? I could have you over and home again within an afternoon. Chrysm will accommodate all my needs, and that includes sedu transport for the models I wish to work with.'

I had no idea what he was talking about. 'It's really up to my guardians,' I said. 'Perhaps you should speak to them.'

'We can *pay*,' Sabarah said frostily.

Anxiously, I glanced about, looking for Malakess. He was still engaged in conversation with the Hegemon. I put out a plea in mind touch, and at once Malakess turned and caught my eye. In that moment, something happened. Everything in the room seemed to go out of focus but for Malakess's eyes. I gulped air, as if I'd surfaced from drowning.

Malakess excused himself from his companions and came to my side. 'I'm sorry to drag Gesaril from you,' he said to the artist, 'but there are some introductions we have to make. Please excuse us.'

He took my arm and led me away. 'Are you all right?'

'No. No, I'm not.'

'Damn Gelaming. What did he threaten you with?'

'Painting me.'

'Hmm, oh well, you're unscathed. Dinner will be served soon. I think we can talk to somehar else now, don't you?'

Suddenly, I was in a daze, confused and befuddled. What had happened? I was introduced to hara whose faces were mere blurs to me, whose voices were like the twittering of birds. I felt hot, sick and yet incredibly elated at the same time.

Presently, Iscane came into the salon and announced loudly that dinner was ready to be served and would we all please proceed to the dining hall. Malakess took my arm again. 'You look very hot,' he said. 'Are you all right?'

'Yes, yes, just hot.'

'Don't let the Gelaming bother you. They were bound to target you. Grow a thick skin, Gesaril. You're going to need it.'

Hara were moving past us back into the hall, on the way to the dining area. I felt as if they were swiftly moving shadows and Malakess and I were held in a pool of stillness. 'They want me to go to Immanion.'

'Not surprising. You *will* go. I'll take you sometime. Life doesn't begin and end for you here in Alba Sulh. You're destined for bigger things.'

Unaccountably, tears welled in my eyes. Malakess brushed away the overspill that ran down my cheeks. 'Hey,' he murmured. 'Don't be overwhelmed. Be an ambassador for your tribe.' He held my face in his hands and kissed my brow.

As he drew away from me, I saw Iscane staring at us, his wide-eyed expression that of a riled cat. If he'd had fur, it would be fluffed out. I took a step back. 'I'm fine... honestly. Let's go.'

The dining hall was immense. There were two long tables running down either side of the room, and a high table at top, where of course Malakess held a place of honour. The Nagini had so far deigned not to show themselves, but now made an appearance. Malakess said this was because they wanted to make it clear that they were not in Kyme for the party or to meet Gelaming.

They were guests of the Sulh, it was dinner time, so they came to join us for the meal. I have never seen such exotic hara before. Their clothes were very colourful and their dark skins were like creamy coffee. Some wore turbans, while others affected complicated hairstyles. A few wore their hair long and straight, although the partings on their heads were coloured red or gold. Their jewellery was ostentatious, but I thought it looked wonderful. Some had delicate filigree chains attached to nose rings and earrings, and the skin of their hands and arms were painted with complicated patterns, which Malakess told me was henna. They moved softly and graciously like cats, and their eyes were beautifully shaped, what you call almond-shaped, outlined in kohl. They wore jewels stuck upon the centre of their brows and their voices were gentle and melodious, although only a few of them could speak our language. They seemed like dehara, creatures of myth.

I took my place beside Malakess at the top table with the leaders of the Nagini and Sulh of high rank. The Kymian phyle leader was present, the illustrious Poltenemy, who I had never seen before. He greeted me in a distant manner, and then devoted himself entirely to the Nagini. One of them sat on Malakess's other side, so I was able to listen in to their conversation. It appeared that only a few of the delegation had graced the dinner. No second generation Nagini was present. I was eaten up with curiosity. I wanted to meet one of those younger hara. I had presumed the Nagini would be ascetic and distant, but this was not the case. They were perfectly affable with the Sulh and other tribes, maintaining their disdain for the Gelaming alone. Haruah, who sat next to Malakess, drank wine like any other har and then, before the dessert was brought in, showed us some conjuring tricks. He had a diamond set into one of his teeth, which glittered when he smiled. His jet black hair hung loose over his shoulders and was braided with golden beads. He was also first generation, and knew our language perfectly. I'd drunk more wine than I should have done by then, and said, 'Will you teach me your magic?'

Haruah grinned. 'Not magic, tiahaar, just illusion. Nohar learns the magic of the Nagini.'

Malakess laughed. 'You are using on it us even now, my friend, aren't you?'

Haruah gave Malakess a smouldering glance. 'If you perceive so, then no. If I were, you would not be able to tell.'

'Your magic is very strong,' Malakess said.

I realised at that point that my presence might well become superfluous very soon. This depressed me. My mind was in such a spin, I wasn't sure why exactly. When Malakess had met my eyes across a room, it had touched me. Did I desire him? Was that it? Why couldn't I work out what I was feeling? One thing was obvious. I could not compete with this specimen of harish perfection now bewitching Malakess with his subtle magic. I felt about two years old.

Some time later, Malakess left the table to visit the bathroom. Haruah reached out and took hold of one of my hands. 'It is only play,' he said softly.

'What is, tiahaar?'

He laughed and squeezed my fingers. 'Do not drink any more.' He winked. 'Trust me.'

I felt my face grow hot, but put down the wine glass. 'I don't think... I don't think I can do...' I shook my head.

'Then don't think,' said Haruah. He paused. 'You will meet my son.'

'Thank you, I'd like that.'

Another grin. 'Oh, nothing to do with me, tiahaar.

Nothing at all.' It had not been an invitation but a foretelling. How strange.

It must have been well after two in the morning by the time Malakess decided we should leave. Actually getting out of the building took some time. Malakess was waylaid every few steps and had to arrange to have lunch, afternoon tea and then dinner with various Gelaming and Nagini. Sabarah, it was decided, would come to Huriel's house to make sketches of me. My feet were aching, even though we'd been sitting down for most of the night, and my head was still half in some other dimension. The cool dark interior of Malakess's carriage was a relief. I sighed and leaned back against the cushions.

'You did very well,' Malakess said as we began the journey home. 'I know it was exhausting, but you were a credit to Kyme and to me.'

I grunted in response. The thought of my bed was the most delicious thing imaginable, or was it? Part of me was tired and aching, but another part was alert and panting for action. That part wanted to leap out of the carriage and run all the way home or perhaps away across the hills beyond Kyme. I could become a deer and just run for ever.

'Gesaril?'

I opened my eyes and glanced at Malakess. What did he think of me really? Only a couple of weeks ago, I'd been affronted at the thought he might desire me, but now I thought he didn't and that was somehow worse. Huriel had been right, it seemed. 'What?'

He pulled a quizzical face. 'You seem... strange.'

I put a hand over my eyes. 'I am strange, yes.' I lowered my hand. 'You could have sent me home alone, you know. I wouldn't have minded.'

He smiled. 'I am not a har to rush things.'

What did that mean?

'The Nagini are subtle,' he continued. 'But I am not as gullible as they think.'

'Haruah is like a dehar,' I said. 'I can imagine him dancing, all in veils, which drop off one by one. By the final veil, you will nearly be dead with longing.'

Malakess laughed. 'Striking imagery, Gesaril! But remember, the Nagini are named for serpent spirits. Handle with care if you don't wish to be bitten, or constricted to death!'

'A bite from a Nagini… hmm. I imagine it would take you to a world of dreams.'

Again, Malakess laughed. 'You like them, don't you. I think perhaps you should meet some of the younger ones.'

'I'm told I will do.' I swallowed, and it felt as if my throat were full of sand. 'But maybe it is not the Nagini who *inspire* me, as our friend tiahaar Sabarah would say. Maybe it is somehar else.'

Malakess was silent, and a ringing tension filled the interior of the carriage. I shouldn't have said that. Stupid of me.

I opened my mouth to speak again, but Malakess interrupted me. 'You've drunk a lot, Gesaril. I'll take you home.'

'Don't,' I said. 'Take me somewhere else.'

Malakess sighed, rubbed a hand over his mouth. 'I am not Ysobi,' he said.

Again, I was not sure of his precise meaning. He could have thought I wanted to pretend he was Ysobi, or was merely telling me he'd not take advantage of me as Ysobi had. 'I know,' I said. 'You're nothing like him.'

'That's not entirely true,' Malakess said, 'but nevertheless I'm taking you home.'

'Kess...' I had never called him that before. The short form of his name sounded intimate in my mouth.

'No, Gesaril. I won't be responsible for you in this way. Think about what you're suggesting. Tomorrow, you'll feel differently.'

'I won't. I felt this way before I started drinking. That's the truth.'

Malakess hesitated before speaking. 'It would be very easy for me, Gesaril, very easy, but you are young, in turmoil, and under my care. This would be good for neither of us. Now please, say nothing more.'

And so I didn't. We finished the journey in prickly silence. At Huriel's gate I got out of the carriage without speaking and didn't close the door behind me. I wanted Malakess to call me back, but he didn't. I heard him pull the door closed and then the driver urged the horses onward. I stood there listening until I could no longer hear the sound of their hooves.

This morning, I was so full of cringing shame I could barely move. I decided the best option was to stay in bed. I had virtually begged Malakess, one of the highest ranking hara in Kyme, to take aruna with me. How could I bear to continue living? It was too embarrassing to endure. I was used to every har I met desiring me, but Malakess had turned me down. My self-loathing was augmented by the fact I'd drunk so much the night before the effects were still in my body, which was unusual.

Huriel brought me breakfast and, towering over my bed, inspected my pathetic state. 'A harish hangover,' he said. 'That's novel, Gesaril.'

'Leave me alone,' I said and pulled the covers over my head.

'Can't,' Huriel said. 'Malakess has sent a note.

You're to join him for lunch with the Gelaming, or rather *we* are. I'm coming with you.' My heart leapt at the news, but from what emotion it was difficult to tell.

I put my head out of the bed. 'Kess has invited a Gelaming to stay here.'

'I've already heard,' Huriel said darkly. 'Chrysm Luel. He'll report back on us.'

I sat up and picked up a piece of toast from the tray Huriel had laid on the bed. 'I was awful last night,' I said. 'I'm surprised Malakess wants to see me again.'

Huriel's eyebrows shot up. 'Why? What did you do? He didn't mention anything when he called round earlier.'

He'd been here? I tried to swallow the toast in my mouth and had to drink some tea to accomplish the task. 'It's your fault,' I said.

'Mine? How? What on earth happened?'

'I threw myself at your mentor and he declined the offer. I was drunk, of course.'

'Oh...' Huriel pulled a face. 'Oh well, no harm done. I'm glad to hear your libido has woken up.'

'No harm done?' I asked exasperatedly. 'Really, Huriel. He must think me such a fool. He turned me down!'

'He *is* aware of your history,' Huriel said. 'He wouldn't take advantage. He probably thinks you should... get back into yourself, as it were, with somehar nearer your own age.'

'Do you think that? Before, you implied I should take aruna with Malakess, that it would do me good.'

'I don't think it would be a bad thing,' Huriel said, 'but I'm not Malakess. I don't know his reasons for declining your offer, but I'm sure he refused you because he thought it was best for you.' He smiled. 'Only weeks ago you were protesting how much it offended you he might desire you.'

'I'm aware of the irony,' I said. 'I don't know if I can face him today.'

'Of course you can. This invitation is clearly extended to show you all is well.'

'I suppose so.'

Huriel put his head to one side. 'Do you *feel* for Malakess, Gesaril? This isn't an Ysobi replacement thing, is it?'

'I don't *feel* for him, no... not like that. It was physical, that's all.'

'Well, it has been a long time since you last took aruna. You must remedy that as soon as possible.'

'Is that an offer?'

Huriel laughed. 'It seems you are in heat! It wasn't an offer, no. I'm not the har you want, and you know it. Get dressed. We're going out in an hour.'

I dressed myself in another of the expensive costumes Huriel had bought for me and pinned up my hair, allowing a few tendrils to dangle over my face. All the while I got ready, I kept myself in check. I could remember the excitement I'd felt getting ready to go to places where I'd known Ysobi would be. I couldn't fall into the same trap here. I mustn't look upon Malakess as a huge challenge just because he'd spurned me. It would be so easy to do that, and it would end badly. Huriel was right. I must find somehar else, maybe even a Gelaming. But then, it might all go wrong, because of what I'm like. I'm not good with aruna. I realise now that I enjoy the chase and making hara want me, but then it's all too much and I'm scared of pain and bad memories, and I resent the hara for wanting me. It's been such a relief not to feel any of that since I've been in Kyme. Damn harish needs! All because of a glance across a room.

Ridiculous.

We took lunch in the hotel in town where the Gelaming were staying. It was, in fact, an elegant establishment and surely as good as anything in Immanion. Chrysm and his companions were dressed casually and looked much better for it, in my opinion. Malakess was already there with them when Huriel and I arrived. He greeted me as if nothing had happened the night before, and behaved towards me in a manner that suggested he was an unofficial hura to me. It did no good. All I could think about was touching his body, and even the acts of eating and drinking were charged with a sensual current.

'So when are you going to invite me to dinner with the Nagini?' Chrysm asked.

Malakess laughed. 'You presume I can do that? They go their own way. It's up to them.'

'Oh, come on,' Chrysm chided. 'They like you. You could be our advocate and impress upon the Nagini we are not the evil they fear. I'll make no secret of the fact it would be extremely good for me if I could go home with the Nagini under my belt. They should join the confederation of tribes.'

'They would say they have no need of it,' Malakess said. 'I can't put that kind of pressure on them, Chrysm. It's up to you to *seduce* them.'

Chrysm pulled a wry face. 'Perhaps that is the only route. Literally.' He regarded Malakess steadily. 'You want things from me, Kess. Maybe I'm prepared to trade for them.'

Malakess rested his elbows on the table, his chin upon his bunched hands. 'I see. *Now* we get to the main course!'

Chrysm was unabashed. He made a languid gesture with one hand. 'There's no point in dissembling. You want our students and our endorsement. I have persuasive power in the Hegemony. Many of them are unconcerned with the Arts and consider it of minor consequence. I usually get my own way, simply because nohar else is interested in my aims.'

I was surprised Chrysm spoke so openly in front of Huriel and me, even if his fellow Gelaming were already aware of this situation. Chrysm considered us of minor consequence too, it seemed. I caught Huriel's eye and he raised his eyebrows, took a drink of wine. I sensed his frosty disapproval. It was insulting to imply the Sulh could be bought.

'I will arrange a dinner,' Malakess said at last. 'The rest is up to you.'

Huriel sighed, shook his head once, almost imperceptibly, and reached for the wine bottle. Chrysm ignored him, if he'd noticed the gesture, and I have no doubt that he had. 'Excellent, Kess!' He nodded towards me. 'Make it an intimate affair. Bring your beautiful protégé. I noticed tiahaar Haruah took a shine to him.'

That was beyond propriety, but Malakess did not react badly. 'Gesaril, what do you think of that?'

'I can dance on my hind legs and balance a ball on my nose,' I said. I couldn't resist it.

Chrysm laughed. 'That's the spirit!' he said. He raised his glass. 'To mutual success and satisfaction.'

For all his brashness and sometimes inappropriate directness, Chrysm Luel does have a certain appealing manner. He makes you feel included, somehow, part of something important. I don't think Huriel felt that at all, but then Chrysm paid him little attention and clearly considered him of little use other than providing accommodation that might bring him nearer to the Nagini. Chrysm's personal staff would bring his luggage over to Huriel's house tomorrow. The Gelaming were being entertained by the phylarch, Poltenemy that evening.

Once business was concluded, as far as Chrysm was concerned, the conversation turned to idle chat. Chrysm made us laugh a lot. He was quite rude about some of other Hegemons, mimicking their speech and actions. His coterie of artists and writers clearly delighted in this and sucked up to him appallingly.

As the hotel staff cleared away the remains of our meal, Chrysm turned to me. 'It would please me greatly if you'd show me around Kyme this afternoon,' he said.

I knew immediately he had other things on his mind as well, and wasn't sure what to say. Should I accept? There was a huge obstacle I had to jump over in my head and this might be the helping hand I needed. 'Well...' I began.

'I'm sorry, I must deprive you,' Malakess interrupted. 'Gesaril has work to do today.'

'What about my sketches?' Sabarah demanded. Everyhar ignored him.

'Oh, have a heart, my friend,' Chrysm said. 'Give the har a day off.'

Malakess maintained his sweetness. 'I wish I could, but you *do* want us to make arrangements with the Nagini for you, don't you?'

'You know I do,' Chrysm said. He sighed and smiled at me. 'A pity. Oh well, another time. I expect to remain in Kyme for some days.' He stood up and bowed to Malakess. 'Send me word when the arrangements are confirmed. Will it be tonight?'

'I think perhaps tomorrow at the earliest,' Malakess said. 'Give me some time.'

'As you wish.' Chrysm turned to Huriel. 'My staff will bring my effects to your house in the morning. I'll be arriving myself around lunch time. Thank you for your offer. I always feel more at ease in private houses.'

'My pleasure,' Huriel said tightly.

Chrysm jerked his head to his sycophantic group and they trailed out of the dining room after him.

'Pompous, conceited ass!' Huriel declared. 'Really, Kess, I don't know how you can stand pandering to him.'

'I can endure it if it provides a result,' Malakess said. 'Don't let it get to you, Huriel.'

'Suggesting you *give* Gesaril to the Nagini, though... that was outrageous, and an insult to both Sulh and Nagini, not to mention a tremendous slur upon Gesaril himself.'

'It's all right,' I said, laying a hand on Huriel's arm; the flesh and bones were tense beneath my fingers. 'I don't mind. I'll do what's necessary to help.'

'Not *that*, you won't!' Huriel said. 'Don't go near Chrysm Luel, Gesaril. He'll eat you up and spit out the bones.'

'Is that an order, father?' I said sweetly.

'Yes,' Huriel said. 'It's an order, son.'

I glanced at Malakess. What did he think?

'Huriel's right,' Malakess said.

'What do you want me to do this afternoon?' I asked him.

'Nothing. I made that up to excuse you from his company.'

'Oh.'

Malakess turned to Huriel. 'I thought I'd bring Haruah and a couple of his hara to your place tonight. Is that all right?'

'Perfectly,' Huriel said. 'We'll go back at once and inform Rayzie and Ystayne. Do the Nagini have any special dietary requirements?'

'I don't know,' Malakess said. 'But I'll go to the

Academy and find out. They're staying there. One of their hara can come over to you.'

'Excellent. He and my staff can go shopping.' Huriel got to his feet. 'Come along, Gesaril.' He was getting more like a father or hostling at every passing moment.

'See you later,' Malakess said. And that was that. No mention of the previous evening, not a flicker of interest.

Despite what had been said, or not said, at lunch, Sabarah turned up at Huriel's house late this afternoon. Everyhar was busy with preparations for dinner, so I took the Gelaming out into the garden. Here, I sat beneath an apple tree while he made dozens of quick sketches. There were no lascivious undercurrents in Sabarah's behaviour. He really did just want to paint me. He frowned as he worked, his arm moving quickly as he made bold sweeping strokes with his charcoal. I asked him an inane question at one point and he simply uttered: 'sssh!' He liked to work in silence, it appeared. Eventually, he paused to smoke a cigarette and let me look at his drawings.

I was quite shocked by what I saw. I looked winsome, and very young. He had captured pain within my eyes, pain that I thought I hid well. It was discomforting that Sabarah had seen so much in me. 'They are wonderful pictures,' I said. 'I'm not sure if I look like that, though. Can I keep one of them?'

'If you like,' Sabarah said. He grinned. 'Just one of those sketches would sell for quite a lot in Immanion.'

'Thanks! I'll get it framed, if I can, and hang it in my room.'

'I'd like to do a series of pictures,' Sabarah said. 'I can see you in a number of settings and moods. It would make a good show for the spring.'

'I'm really not sure I could come to Immanion,

though,' I said. 'And you couldn't keep coming here, surely?'

Sabarah tapped ash from the end of his cigarette. 'You don't know about sedim, do you?'

I shook my head. 'No, what is it?'

"Not it, *they*,' Sabarah replied. 'They are a form of transport that can cross into the ethers and carry you long distances in a short space of time. That is how we travel. It is also through them that we are able to excel at trade and other things.'

'That's amazing,' I said. 'I'd like to try it.'

Sabarah shrugged. 'Well, perhaps we can arrange it. It's clear your guardians are very protective of you, and so they should be. You'd perhaps need a chaperone.'

It's astounding how your first impressions of a har can change so much. Sabarah was not half as pompous or presumptuous as I'd thought. He seemed quite down to earth now, in fact. Sabarah mistook my silence for something other than reflective thought. He smiled rather sadly. 'I know we Gelaming are not regarded in the best of lights abroad, and sometimes hara like Chrysm do little to dispel the bad reputation. Some question whether it is right to let him represent our tribe. Chrysm is fairly young by Hegemony standards, second generation like you.'

That was another revelation. 'It seemed to me at lunch you all adore him,' I said, wondering at once whether that was a wise thing to say.

Sabarah didn't take offence, however. He smiled. 'Well, let's just say it's in our interests to keep him sweet. He's responsible for all the major shows in Immanion and his patronage can make the difference between poverty and affluence. He's not a bad har, but does tend to put his foot in it. He's not that adept at reading other hara, I'm afraid. But then again...' Sabarah smiled grimly. 'Perhaps he is all too adept.'

'Hmm, I wonder whether he should be let loose on the Nagini, then.'

Sabarah nodded. 'I've wondered the same. Still, it won't affect me, one way or the other.' He stubbed out his cigarette. 'Shall we continue?'

By the end of the sitting, I felt that I'd begun to make a new friend. Sabarah told me he'd like to make more sketches, in different settings, and would begin work on the paintings once he returned to Immanion. I agreed to meet him at his hotel the following day. We could go to any number of locations around the town and the surrounding countryside.

Now, Sabarah has left and I've only got half an hour or so to get ready. Time for another new set of clothes. I could get used to this.

I had wondered whether Haruah would bring his son with him, but perhaps he didn't want to force his prophecy. He came with two friends instead, both of whom knew enough Albish to be able to converse fairly easily with us. It might be that younger Nagini were sequestered away from adult company, with all its risks and perils. I knew nothing of their tribal customs. We gathered in Huriel's sitting room for aperitifs and here Haruah drew me aside to give me a gift. 'I'm pleased to see you here,' he said. 'This is for you.'

It was an article wrapped in red silk and tied with a gold ribbon. I unwrapped it carefully and found within a wooden carving of a strange creature that appeared to be a beautiful har who was half serpent. From the waist down he sat upon thick, reptilian coils. 'Who is it?' I asked.

'That is Nagarana,' Haruah said. 'He is the dehar of Nagini. Keep him by you and he will listen to your prayers. Nagarana knows no tribal boundaries. One day, he will sit beside Aruhani and his brothers in the greatest fanes in the world.'

'Thank you,' I said. 'It's a wonderful gift.'

Haruah smiled widely. 'Nagarana is similar to Aruhani in many ways, being a dehar of aruna, birth and death, among other attributes. Talk to him, my friend.'

I looked into Haruah's eyes. Like Sabarah, clearly he saw all too much of me. I wasn't very clever at hiding my inner self, it seemed. Still, self centred contemplations must be put aside for tonight. It hadn't escaped me that Haruah saw Nagarana as a deity for all hara. That didn't speak of reclusiveness to me, and I certainly didn't pick up the slightest impression that the Nagini hid a desire for world domination in a military sense. Perhaps I was too young and naïve to talk of political things, but I felt comfortable with Haruah, so spoke my mind. 'The Gelaming are impatient to talk to you. I expect you know that.'

'Oh yes.'

'Perhaps you should ask Chrysm to build a temple to Nagarana in Immanion. He is desperate to please you.'

Haruah laughed. 'The temples to Nagarana will be built by ordinary hara, not Hegemons, but your suggestion is amusing.'

There was a comfortable silence for some moments as I examined the little carving, then Haruah reached out and stroked my face. 'Ah, poor Gesaril. You were denied last night, were you not?'

I couldn't help but blush. 'Hmm. I lack the sophisticated wiles of older hara, I think. I give up, to be honest. I will become a hermit.'

'I should take you home with me, then. The lands to the north of our territory are the domain of monks, who live in high, dangerous, inaccessible places. They are hara created from an ancient strain of humanity.'

'What is the name of your country?' I asked.

'Veranaka,' he replied. 'Well, some hara call it by different names. It is a vast land, with a great many tribes.'

I sighed. 'I feel so... uninformed. My whole world consisted of the tiny territory of Lyonis for so long, and yet really the world is vast. I only know of the tribes of Almagabra and Megalithica.'

'That's only natural,' Haruah said. 'During the Changing Times, communication broke down completely between different countries. We all underwent our own traumatic changes. Perhaps now is the time for communication to be rekindled, as long as all concerned respect other cultures.'

'You fear the Gelaming are like humans, don't you?' I said. 'They want everyhar to be Gelaming.'

'That, unfortunately, is the impression they give,' Haruah agreed. 'But Almagabra is small in comparison to the eastern lands. We've kept ourselves to ourselves for many years. Some of us are now interested in looking outwards. We are all privileged to be what we are, united by the common destiny that we were bequeathed by the world. The Nagini believe it is not beyond Wraeththu to embrace each other as brothers, wherever they might live or whatever they might believe.'

'Do all hara in your country feel that way?' I asked.

Haruah pulled a rueful face. 'No, not all.' He smiled. 'Now is not the time for such talk. We are here to make friends and to enjoy ourselves. Perhaps we should rejoin the company.'

As we turned back to everyhar else, I noticed that Malakess was watching me speculatively.

Ystayne and Rayzie had excelled themselves in the kitchen, aided by one of Haruah's staff, a har who could not speak Albish but who nevertheless had communicated well enough in mind touch to work easily with Huriel's staff. The Nagini were curious about our cuisine and wanted to try everything. There was a myriad of things for them to taste, each dish laced fragrantly with local herbs, the meats slathered with berry sauces. The topics of conversation covered over dinner were so vast and so interesting it was like discovering a magical fountain of knowledge. The Nagini had travelled over sea and land to reach us; they did not have transport like the Gelaming. They told us tales of every country they'd visited. So many tribes. So many different kinds of Wraeththu. It unsettled me to realise how little I know of my own kind. Still, I can honestly say I enjoyed the evening far more than the party at the Academy. I was acutely conscious of Malakess's presence, but it felt good rather than uncomfortable. I felt I was shining. Haruah brought out the best in me. He flattered me subtly, winding his magic into my being. But it was not for his benefit.

The Nagini left before midnight, after which Huriel, Malakess and I went back to the sitting room to sit before the fire and drink some pear liqueur that Rayzie had made last year. I felt mellow and drowsy; our little party had been a great success, not least because Malakess had persuaded Haruah to dine with Chrysm the following evening. Huriel and Malakess discussed the evening's events, while I stared into the fire, my mind comfortably numb. I must have fallen asleep, because I was brought to full consciousness by Malakess shaking my shoulder. The fire had died down and I held an empty glass in my hand, sticky with liqueur. 'Wake up,' Malakess said. 'Huriel's gone to bed. So should you... soon.'

I yawned and sat up straight. 'Why are you still here?'

Malakess hesitated, then said, 'I wanted to talk to you.'

'About last night, I suppose.' I sighed. 'I apologise.'

'You don't have to,' Malakess said. 'What is it you want from me, Gesaril? Honestly?'

'Nothing...' I shook my head. 'Well, perhaps it's obvious. And you think I look on you and see Ysobi. I told you that, once. It's not very flattering, I know, but it's not the case now.'

'I don't want to make your problems any worse.'

'Oh, I'm sick of my problems!'

Again, Malakess paused. 'What are they exactly,

anyway? Will you tell me?'

'Well, apart from a swarm of emotional disaster areas, I have a physical problem with soume.'

'Physical problem... what do you mean?'

'I think it's physical. I'm not sure. Anyway, it hurts me and sometimes causes damage.'

'You should see a physician.'

'I think it's too late for that.'

'But you're har. Your body should have repaired itself fully.'

'Then maybe it's not a real problem after all. I don't know. I had pelki committed on me when I was very young. It's hardly surprising that caused fallout, is it?'

Malakess shook his head. 'No...'

'And yet despite this problem, I've spent most of my post feybraiha life being what somehar in Jesith called a soume shrew. A predator. And I have been. I don't deny it. It was the only way I could feel, I think, having hara want me, especially those who were already chesna with somehar else. Then, when I'd got them hooked, it always went wrong, for obvious reasons.' I looked into Malakess's eyes. 'I've changed a lot. I understand myself more, but even so, that understanding doesn't make the problem go away.'

'How do you know that?'

'Well...' Actually, I didn't.

'I will try with you, Gesaril, if that's what you still want.'

I stared at him like an idiot for some moments. 'What?'

'We must have an understanding,' he said. 'I don't want you being hurt, in an emotional sense.'

This was too much to take in, and totally unexpected. I didn't know how to react. Was Haruah's magic so strong? 'I don't know what to say.' Despite that, I reached out and took one of his hands, held on to it as if I was drowning and he was the lifeline to land. Twice I'd felt this way with him. He let me crush his fingers for a short time, which must have hurt, then drew me to him. We shared breath for several minutes, azure skies yawning in my head. It was like flying. I remembered the first time I'd shared breath with Ysobi, how I'd felt I was in a scarlet and black temple, and I was the altar there. By that time, we'd taken aruna together many times.

Malakess drew away from me, kissed my brow. 'Let's go upstairs.'

I felt so nervous and tense I could barely walk. This was what I wanted, wasn't it? Or did I just want the chase again, the longing in a har's eyes?

I took Malakess to my room. It occurred to me that Huriel had spoken to him about me, and that was why he'd sloped off to bed to leave us alone. Maybe now, he lay awake, listening for sounds. Malakess and I undressed in silence, and all the while I kept getting flashbacks to Jesith. It wasn't pleasant. I remembered the phylarch's house, Ysobi coming to me there in the night, when were supposed not to see each other. I could smell the fragrance of his hair.

I sat down on the bed and put my face in my hands. I was not simply haunted, I must be possessed. Malakess came to me, squatted before me and put a hand on my shoulder. 'Gesaril?'

'I want to forget, but I can't,' I said.

'Maybe you're not ready yet,' he said softly.

I rubbed my temples. 'Maybe not.'

'Get into bed. It's okay. Just rest.'

I hadn't even looked at him yet. Still averting my eyes, I pulled the blankets over me and he climbed in beside me. I lay with my back to him and he curled his arms round me, pulled me close. 'Just sleep,' he said.

The song of birds in the creepers outside my window woke me up. It must have been very early in the morning. Malakess slept beside me, lying on his back, his hair spread all over the pillows. I propped myself up on an elbow to study him. It was easy this way, while he slept. He wore an amulet around his neck. I lifted it and the stone was warm from the heat of his body. I ran my hand over his smooth skin and he made a small sound, arched his back a little, but he didn't wake up. I pulled back the covers and gazed upon him. Who was this har, really? Who had he loved, who had he lost? What went on in his inner life? I hardly knew him. Asleep, he looked vulnerable and young, far from the contained High Codexia I'd first met. At heart, he was har. He had lived through the early days of Wraeththu with all their horrors and triumphs. He had probably killed humans and even other hara. I wondered about his inception, his history. Suddenly, all the experience contained within him made him more beautiful to my eyes. This frame, this perfect form, all that we are. The High Codexia, in essence, did not exist. It was a construct, a mask. What did exist was Malakess, his mind and body, his spirit. In dreams, he too ran over the hills like a deer, and politics and intrigue could not possibly exist. In dreams, he was free. And I could share that.

My hand hovered over his belly. What could possibly be so terrifying about another harish body? His ouana-lim, crude though it seems to say it, was not as large as Ysobi's and seemed less threatening, less like a weapon. But I still shrank from touching it. I didn't want it to wake up. Perhaps I should cover him up again before he got cold and woke up himself. But something stopped me. Maybe there were some hurdles I couldn't leap at the moment, but I could at least take aruna again, on my terms, and with this secret creature, unmasked in sleep.

I leaned over to share breathe with him and sensed his mind rise from slumber. He put his arms around me and returned the sharing. I reached down to caress his soume-lam and he parted his legs for me. My mind must remain focused in the present moment. I was here, now, not in the past. But still, those hated images came back to me: Ysobi writhing beneath my touch, my awe at his beauty, the desire to enter him and the final consummation of that desire. I was just on the brink of pulling away from Malakess completely, a cruel and inconsiderate thing to do, seeing as I'd now thoroughly aroused him, but before I could do so, he took hold of my hand and pulled it away himself. He'd seen into my mind. I thought he might be angry or at least disappointed, but he merely rolled me onto my back and continued to share breath with me. The flavour of it had changed. I pulled away. 'No...'

'Hush,' he said. 'Trust me, Gesaril. I'll not have your ghosts on my back as well as yours. Relax and trust me. I'll not hurt you, I swear it.'

I let myself go limp. I'd believe him and hope that was magic enough to make it real. *Nagarana,* I prayed, *I don't know you yet, but be with me now...*

So many times I thought, *Now is the moment, now he'll touch me, open me up*, but each time I was wrong. He concentrated on my skin, stroking gently, and on filling me with his soothing breath. I could feel his ouana-lim hot against me, eager to go about its business, but still he held back. I reached out to take him in my hand, but he took hold of my fingers. He guided us together to my own body, and together we touched gently that shrinking heart of me that feared pain. He did not invade me, but held my hand, directed it. I went into myself, at first passive, and then gradually, as desire was kindled, I caressed the areas inside me that were the most sensitive to touch. Malakess held on to my wrist, his mouth still against my own. The tides of aruna were rising. I was slippery and hungry. Malakess took hold of my arms and lifted them above my head, his fingers laced with mine. Before I realised it, he'd slid inside me, and it didn't hurt. It didn't hurt at all.

The one thing I'd forgotten about, or possibly had never fully experienced before, was the spiritual nourishment that aruna bestows. When Malakess and I finally went down to breakfast, I couldn't feel the ground beneath my feet. My body felt made of light and my mind was utterly at peace, so much so, it brought home to me how wound up and anxious I'd been before. After we'd taken aruna, I'd wept for some time, in relief and wonder and sheer release. I felt as if I'd been freed from a curse.

In the dining room, Huriel held himself under considerable restraint and didn't utter a word, although there was laughter in his eyes. I kept dropping cutlery and knocking things over, as if I'd lost control of my body. Again, Huriel shortly left us alone, as he'd begun his breakfast before we had. I looked upon the har beside me, buttering his toast, and wondered how I felt about him now. What would happen next? Would there be a next time? Nothing had been said aloud. We'd spoken with our bodies, that was all.

'What have you got planned today?' Malakess asked me.

'Nothing,' I replied. 'Huriel hasn't told me to do anything in particular. Oh, I have to meet Sabarah later.'

'You will of course come to dinner at the hotel tonight?'

'I will?'

Malakess looked up from his toast and smiled at me. 'I would like you to.'

'Yes, then. Yes, I'd like it too.'

He adopted a serious expression. 'How do you feel now, Gesaril?'

I grinned at him. 'I feel like a dehar, or that I've been possessed by a dehar.'

Malakess shook his head. 'I'm sure you over-rate my skills.' In those words hung the ghost of Ysobi again, the skilled Hienama of arunic arts. I didn't think Malakess had intended it, but that's what I heard.

'It depends what you mean by skill,' I said. 'I think compassion is worth more than skill.'

Malakess stared at the table for some moments. Then he drew a breath. 'I have to ask you something. Please speak honestly. Do you regard last night as a one off occasion?'

I stared at him, even though he wouldn't meet my eyes. 'That depends entirely on how you feel about it.'

He laughed, rather nervously, and then looked at me. 'I feel good about it. I don't know where this will lead us, Gesaril. I think we should just see what happens, but I want you to know that I'd like us to remain close. I think... we go well together.' He groaned and shook his head. 'Seductive talk is not one of my virtues.'

'I understand you perfectly,' I said. 'I think we want the same thing.'

'But I'm so much older than you...'

'Aruna does not recognise age,' I said. 'When we were together, it didn't matter. I didn't even think about it. You were just a beautiful har, that's all. I felt comfortable with you, in every sense, and that's rare for me. I'm not about to let that go.'

He nodded. 'These things, new bonds, are fragile. We need to take care.'

No second generation har would ever say such a thing, but then we were all young in comparison to hara like Malakess.

I knew already that Malakess was not the kind of har who would appreciate overt gestures of intimacy in public places, nor would he be spontaneous to offer affection. To him, aruna was a private matter, and intimate bonds between hara should not be part of a display. I liked the thought of that. We would be like a secret, but not a shameful one, such as that I'd shared with Ysobi.

Now I have to go and meet Sabarah. What new wonders will tonight bring? I can't believe how much my life has changed, how different I feel. I have to write something every day. I don't want to forget any of this.

Miyacalasday, Ardourmoon 24

Sabarah sensed at once something different about me and must have guessed another har was the cause. He didn't question me about it, but was pleased I radiated a different kind of energy today, that he would attempt to capture in his sketches. I floated through the day, waiting only for the night. Even the meal with the Gelaming seemed just like a delaying nuisance. I wanted to be close to Malakess again.

The only hara present at the meal was a delegation of five Nagini, Chrysm Luel, Malakess and myself. Chrysm behaved himself quite well in front of the Nagini, and didn't appear to offend them. He spoke earnestly of how the greatest tribes should co-operate in order to help the weaker tribes who needed support. 'I know how Gelaming appear to others,' he said, (as if he'd been coached by Sabarah, to be honest), 'and that the Hegemony is renowned for its arrogance, but like you the Gelaming have only the welfare of Wraeththu at heart, and the welfare of the world itself.'

It was a credit to Chrysm that he sounded sincere while saying that.

Haruah and his companions listened patiently to everything the Hegemon said. It wasn't possible to gauge their reaction, because they kept it hidden, but I had no doubt some private dialogue took place between them in mind touch.

'I think perhaps we could talk about trade,' Haruah said carefully. 'There we might find mutual benefit.' Clearly, the Nagini were going to proceed cautiously and see if the Gelaming could prove themselves.

'Of course,' Chrysm said smoothly, 'although that's not my realm of expertise. You should speak with the Hegemony Chancellor, Tharmifex Calvel, and of course the Tigrons and Tigrina. It would give me great pleasure to be able to arrange a meeting.'

Haruah nodded. 'Allow us time to discuss the matter in private,' he said. 'But, seeing as we're already in your part of the world, it would make sense to visit Almagabra once our visit here is concluded.'

I don't know how Chrysm prevented himself from leaping from his seat with a victorious, air-thumping shout, but he merely inclined his head. 'It would appear to make sense, yes. I'll be around here for a while longer too. If you would like to discuss anything with me, I'm at your disposal.'

I sincerely hoped that Malakess would get all he wanted from the Gelaming after this.

Once the formal business was concluded, the conversation became more casual and I was able to speak to Haruah in relative privacy. 'I see Nagarana has worked on your behalf already,' Haruah said, grinning widely.

'He has indeed,' I replied. 'Thank you, tiahaar.'

'Learn from the past,' the Nagini said, his expression suddenly intense. My skin prickled.

'I will, tiahaar.'

'I mean it, Gesaril. Do not repeat mistakes, and do not mistake events, and do not drape the present in the robes of lost days.'

He spoke so fiercely, it was like a warning, as if he could see something in my future. 'Tiahaar?' I asked cautiously, hoping he would offer more.

Haruah shook his head, then smiled again. 'No, the world is light for you now. Enjoy it.'

That night, I again took Malakess to my bed, and felt that I exorcised forever the malevolent ghost of Ysobi. New experiences were imprinted over my bad or painful memories. I saw a different side of Malakess, when he became utterly soume for me. He was almost coquettish, certainly playful, so that I actually felt older than him. A new me was emerging too. I could look back on the past and see myself as something like a larva; I was the dragon fly now with spreading iridescent wings. I dined with Hegemons and phylarchs from powerful tribes. I held my own in conversation and was respected.

As much as I try not to think it, I wish that Ysobi knew about this. I want him to see me now, what I've become, so that I can turn my back on him; supposing I could do that.

Pelfazzarsday, Ardourmoon 28

As if the universe has heard me, this morning I have received some contact from Jesith in the form of a letter from, of all hara, Jassenah. It was a long, friendly letter, which surprised me, full of anecdotes about hara I'd known in the town. He thanked me warmly for the gift I'd sent. I noticed though that he didn't mention Ysobi. He must have talked about everyhar in Jesith *but* for Ysobi, in fact. I was tempted to write back at first, but then remembered Haruah's words and stopped myself doing it. I mustn't open that door to the past. If a correspondence develops between Jassenah and myself, it could not be good for me. It's a connection, however tenuous, with Ysobi. If I can't let Jassenah go, I can't let Ysobi go. So there it is: I must remain silent and not respond.

But thinking about letters has made me realise I've not contacted my parents for some time. Neither have they contacted me, of course. Perhaps they've forgotten about me, lost in their dreamy realms. To remind them I exist, I'm going to write a long letter to them now, telling them about the Nagini and the Hegemon and my life in Kyme.

There… it's done. As I was writing it, I considered how harlings are supposed to be close to their parents, but I've never been close to mine. They're not cruel, or even negligent, but I'm not like them and have never been able to share their fairyland world. We don't connect. I suppose they've been cruel and negligent without intending to be. They never recognised my pain, and certainly never helped me deal with it. Perhaps that's what I should have been writing to them about.

Chrysm only stayed in Huriel's house for two days, but he certainly livened the place up for that short time. Now that he'd got the Nagini under his belt, as it were, and a visit to Immanion had been scheduled – complete with sedu transport, which must surely impress even the unimpressionable Nagini – he didn't want to hang around too long. The Nagini made a big gesture to the Sulh too, in that they would leave four of their second generation hara in Kyme to study at the Academy. These young hara are cloistered away in the Academy towers, and from what little Malakess has told me about the arrangement, it appears that chaperones have been left with the students and that they will not be mixing too freely with the rest of us. I've been so enraptured by my relationship with Malakess that I haven't give these students much thought. Although Malakess likes to be fairly private about our union, he did relax enough to put his arm around me in the evenings, when we sat and talked with the Hegemon in Huriel's sitting room. Chrysm was an entertaining har, and even Huriel warmed to him slightly, I think, much to his own disgust. Chrysm definitely realised that it would be inappropriate to flirt with me, because he never spoke to me in such a way again. Malakess stayed at the house every night too.

One time, as we lay in bed, wrapped in each other's arms, I said, 'We could stay at your house too, Kess. You don't have to come here every time.'

'It's far more comfortable here,' he replied.

'Then maybe you should think about making your own house more comfortable.' In those words, I knew, was the subtle implication that if our relationship continued, we would become chesna, and would live together.

'There's plenty of time,' Malakess said. 'I've never really cared about houses.'

I didn't feel I could pursue the subject. Perhaps Malakess is being cautious, waiting to see whether it's possible for us to become chesna. The relationship is still so new. We still don't really know one another, because we haven't shared our histories. As for me, who vowed never to fall in love again, I don't feel the same hot passion for Malakess that I once felt for Ysobi, even though physically we are in tune. For Malakess, aruna is a ritual, an act of reverence. He treats my body as if it were some fragile sacred artefact, almost worships it, but once out of the bedroom, he becomes reserved and somewhat inhibited. I understand the boundaries of our relationship, and it's fine by me. I feel secure and the idea of being the consort of a high ranking har is not without its appeal. If I'm going to do something with my life, why not go for the best here in Kyme?

The Gelaming went home, taking the majority of the Nagini with them. It seems the future looks hopeful for relations between the tribes. We all went back to work, but I spent more time with Malakess, learning about the administration of the library and its projects. He took me to see it, the vast underground labyrinth that was a repository of vast human knowledge and would become, so he hoped, equally full of Wraeththu knowledge. The library had a printing press, which although primitive by later human standards, could produce books. Malakess wanted to encourage hara to write, particularly about the past, the early days of our kind. We talked about this as we roamed around the maze of book stacks. 'Will you write a book?' I asked him.

He pulled a sour face. 'I don't get the time.'

'But you have a history.'

'Yes, who doesn't?'

'I would like to know about it.'

He laughed. 'Oh, you yearn to unearth the reeking corpses of my past!'

'You have reeking corpses in it, then?'

He put an arm about me, drew me onward. 'Not particularly. I'm fairly boring by Wraeththu standards.'

'I don't believe that! Tell me about what it was like in the early days.'

He grimaced. 'All right, a little. We used to discourage visits from hara outside Alba Sulh. We wanted to be mysterious and self-contained. It was a fantasy we had. It didn't last long in the face of reality.'

'You mean in the face of the Gelaming.'

'Mostly. I was incepted fairly late, really. Hara had already begun to produce harlings, and the main communities had been established. I wasn't there at the beginning. The hara who were are the ones who should be writing books.'

'You were human once,' I said. 'That's strange to me. I'd like to know about it.'

'I can't remember much about it,' he said. 'I was incepted young.'

Even I knew that inceptions had rarely taken place before a human child was in their teens. How could he forget all those years of memories? I didn't believe him. Still, if he didn't want to talk about it, that was that. I could perhaps claw out further disclosures as time went on.

I'd been thinking about the Sulh's history as a whole quite a lot and wondered why there was only one tribe on our island, given that originally it had comprised several different human races. At one time, there must have been more tribes, but the Sulh had gained supremacy to become a nation rather than just a tribe, even though we still referred to ourselves as such. This intrigued me. There were certainly no books written about that yet. 'Were there wars?' I asked Malakess.

'Yes,' he answered. 'There were always wars. The Sulh actually comprise several different major tribes who considered it best to ally.'

'Do any of the other tribes still exist?'

'To a degree, yes. They keep to themselves mostly, in inaccessible regions. And there are always the unthrist, the small groups of rogue hara, who ally to no tribe.'

I was of course horribly and intimately familiar with such types.

Agavesday, Mistmoon 29

Well, it's been a few months since the Gelaming and Nagini left Kyme, and I've got lazy with my writing again. I suppose this is because life continues now in the vein it began when Malakess and I got together. I spend most of my time with him, and it's pleasant. Is that a good word to use?

It's strange how I have less of a desire to write now that I feel fairly content. Also, I've been kept very busy. The truth is I *am* writing, but it's for my education, and has no place here. Huriel has started work with me on my caste ascension. Soon I'll undertake the Brynie initiation, and that is the first tier of my training complete. It's helping me to understand myself more and I feel in control. This is the training I should have received in Jesith. I can throw myself into the work and this time it's so much easier, because there are no distractions. If Ysobi's face arises before my inner eye, I can turn my back on it now. It must be over. It must be.

Anyway, the reason I've come back to my account is that there's an event on the horizon: the phylarch of Kyme is to have a birthday party. This is not to celebrate the day his human mother gave him life, but his inception, which he considers to be his true birth. All the local dignitaries will be invited, as well as a few high ranking hara from nearby phyles. I've received a personal invitation to the event, which demonstrates that my relationship with Malakess is known and approved of by – at the very least - the phylarch's social secretary.

The season has turned and the cold winter months

crawl upon us. Snow has come early this year and already a fine dusting mantles the town. Furnaces are roaring in the cellars of the largest houses. Malakess has presented me with a fur-trimmed jacket, covered in embroidery. It's a beautiful thing. I feel sure, and so does Huriel because we've discussed it, that it's only a matter of time before Malakess makes a formal proposal that we should announce a chesna bond. After that, we think it's most likely I'll move into his house.

In fact, only yesterday we talked about it at breakfast. 'Malakess has for some time talked about the idea of having a har to share his life and his responsibilities,' Huriel said. 'He just hasn't found anyhar suitable before.'

'And you think I'm suitable?' I teased.

Huriel smiled, buttering his toast. '*He* thinks so.'

'Has he said as much?'

Huriel took a bite of toast. 'No, but we're old friends. I know.'

As to how this conversation made me feel, it's difficult to tell. In one way, becoming chesna with Malakess seems a natural and preordained certainty. In others, I'm not so sure. It seems too easy. But do I only think this because of what happened in Jesith?

Malakess and I don't sleep together every night, but I'm alone only for about three of every seven. I haven't set eyes on his assistant Iscane since the Academy party, but I think he must be aware of my attachment to Malakess. I sometimes wonder how he feels about it. I've only met the har a couple of times, which I suppose is quite odd, but on both occasions, Iscane oozed dislike. He must be jealous concerning his territory and his position. However, if I'm destined to move into Malakess's house as his chesnari, Iscane will have no choice but to put up with it. I must admit that the thought of a formal bonding with Malakess, even if it isn't as profound as a blood bond, *is* strangely erotic. I fantasise about us having a ceremony, during which I'll sneak out to go to the bedroom. He'll follow me there discreetly and we'll do things to each other that we've never done. By all the dehara, I'm even thinking in terms of harlings – not because I want one, but because I know the aruna that creates them is the most rare and potent kind.

I wonder if I could dare to let down my defences and love this har who has moved me physically so powerfully. I realise I'm holding back emotionally, afraid of being hurt. But surely, once we've announced to the world we're a pair, it will be safe to fall back into Aruhani's waiting arms, let myself open in every sense to the har who would share my life.

Miyacalasday, Adkayamoon 4

I've had to let a few days pass before I've been able to write again. It makes me wince to read over the words I last wrote. How the capricious dehara conspire to trick us!

On the night of the party, Malakess came to collect me in his carriage and this time, as we travelled together in comfortable silence, he held my hand and I sat beside him rather than opposite.

When we arrived at Poltenemy's manse, some miles out of town, I noticed that there were a lot of other second generation hara present, mostly friends of the phylarch and his chesnari's son. These were hara with whom I had never come into contact before. I was not really surprised that they were slightly territorial and appeared to view me as an interloper, if their rather hostile inspections were anything to go by. I decided the best ploy was to keep my head down and stay by Malakess's side. But it was impossible to do that for every single moment, and there came a time when I went alone to the bathroom, a sumptuously appointed room on the first floor. When I came out, a har my own age was standing outside the door. I assumed he wished to use the facilities and inclined my head to him. To my surprise, he grabbed hold of my arm to prevent me leaving.

'We must talk,' he said.

I didn't know him, and had no idea what he might want, but it was clear this wasn't a friendly overture. 'About what?' I asked, pulling my arm away from his grip.

'You won't get away with your tricks here, har. We know about you.'

'Excuse me?'

'You think that Malakess can be your Ysobi here, but we won't let that happen.'

Those words virtually froze my blood. Indeed, this har *knew* about me. 'I have no idea what you're talking about,' I said, determined to keep my dignity. I made to walk off again, but he dragged me back.

'What is it with little shits like you?' he snapped. 'You see somehar happy and you want to ruin it. You think you're so fucking lovely that everyhar will fall at your feet. And the older ones are stupid. They fall for it every time. Well, we're on to you, har. If you think you can get away with your usual scam here, forget it.'

My heart was beating really fast now. I felt slightly dizzy, but had to retain an outward coolness. 'I really have no idea what you're talking about. What exactly am I ruining?'

The har bared his teeth at me. 'How about the life and sanity of Malakess's chesnari? As if you don't know!'

I must have done a double take. 'What? What do you mean? He hasn't got a chesnari.'

'You think?' The har laughed cruelly. 'Oh, you know all right. The moment you saw Malakess you set your sights on him. We watched it happening.'

'But who is this har who's supposed to be chesna with Malakess?' I couldn't believe this might be true. He spent nearly all his time with me. I'd never seen him with somehar else, and surely Huriel would have known and mentioned it.

The har grinned at me without humour. 'Iscane, of course. You know that.'

'Iscane?' I couldn't help laughing, but stopped quickly, because the har looked like he was about to punch me. 'Since when has Malakess been chesna with Iscane?'

'They've lived together for four years,' the har said. 'Now, Iscane's bed is empty of Malakess half the week. He's suffering, but he won't say anything, because he's loyal to Malakess, because he loves him. I have no such scruples. I'll speak my mind. Do the right thing for once and back off, otherwise your life here will be a misery. Trust me.'

I couldn't have felt more dazed if the har *had* physically punched me. This couldn't be true. Life could not be so cruel. 'I don't believe you,' I said. 'Get out of my way.'

The har blocked my path and I saw from the corner of my eye that three other hara had arrived, slinking from the shadowy corridor to the right. My body was filled with the imperative to flee. I knew I was in danger, and it brought back horrific memories from my childhood. Helplessness, fear, the knowledge that whatever I did, I couldn't make the situation better. Anger and hatred oozed from these hara. Before I could bolt, one of them grabbed me from behind, held onto my arms painfully hard. 'Don't piss yourself,' the first har said. 'We won't hurt you... yet. We just want to make ourselves clear.'

I was so frightened then, all I could think of was self-preservation. It reminded me too painfully of what I'd gone through as a harling; strong arms holding me down, the threat and then the reality of physical pain. The implications of what I'd learned would sink in later. 'I didn't know about Iscane,' I said. 'Truly. I didn't know. I've done nothing intentionally.'

The first har hesitated, unsure. He must have been able to tell I spoke the truth, because my words were heart-felt. 'Well,' said the one who held me. 'Whether you knew or not before, you know now.'

The first har nodded. 'That's right. Malakess will never throw Iscane out, har. You'll never have him completely, and Iscane has good friends, lots of them. So, if you want an easy life, just move on to some other poor fool. I'm sure there are enough first generation hara here in Kyme to keep you busy for a few months.'

Their hostile words and stares, the contempt in which they held me, was like a physical force crushing my body. I was back in Jesith, Jassenah standing over my bed. *If you want to drown, then do so. I'll watch from the edge of the bottomless pool.* The first har came close to me, so that I could smell his breath, the tart reek of wine. He was a beautiful creature himself, but his beauty was disfigured by the grimace on his face. He thrust out a hand and grabbed me between the legs. I let out a cry.

'That is nothing,' he said, letting go. 'Stay away from Malakess. Stay away from us. Better still, leave Kyme. We don't want your kind here. We look out for each other.' Now, he grabbed hold of my face, squeezed tightly. It felt as if my heart had stopped beating. What could I do? What could I say? Beg, plead with them?

'Nasander!' one of the other hara said in a warning tone. 'Let him go. You've said what we wanted him to hear.'

The one named Nasander held on to me for a few seconds more, then released me, but the other har still held my arms.

'Borlis,' said my unexpected champion, who I could not see. 'You too. A warning is one thing, but more than that will only get us in trouble.'

My arms were released.

'We're watching you,' Nasander said, pointing a finger right in my face.

Somehow, perhaps through the agency of Nagarana,

I pulled myself together. I wouldn't let these hara see me wretched. 'I don't know what gossip you've heard about me,' I said stiffly, 'but you don't know me, and you can't make assumptions. I've been led to believe Malakess had no chesnari. If what you say is true - and I will make my own investigations obviously - then I will be as affronted as Iscane is. You can insult me, but that doesn't change the fact that Malakess wanted to be with me. That is what your friend Iscane should think about, as will I.' I inclined my head. 'Good evening to you.'

I walked down the stairs, head held high, even though I was terrified they'd fall upon me and tear me apart. But this time, nohar hauled me back. My mind was a whirling vortex; I couldn't think straight. *This can't be true.* My memories were drawn back inexorably to the time when I'd been interviewed by the Jesith phylarch Sinnar. *Gesaril, you must tell me the truth. What's been going on between you and Ysobi?* Sinnar, Jassenah's friend. He'd not been brutal with me, but the distaste in his eyes had been like a slap. *It would be best if you didn't see Ysobi for now.*

Could history really repeat itself like this? Was it possible Malakess had this secret chesnari? If so, what had he intended with me? It became clear to me now that this might be the reason why Malakess always comes to me at Huriel's, and why he is reluctant to talk about his home. I was shocked that so fine and upstanding a har could be so underhand. It wasn't that I expected Malakess to have no other aruna partners apart from me, but a chesnari was a different matter. And yet it had been me who had accompanied Malakess to this party, and me who had received my own invitation to the event, not Iscane. Nothing made any sense, but I had bruises on my arms now, and my ouana-lim was aching where Nasander had cruelly squeezed it. Those hara would not have confronted me like that unless what they'd told me was true.

I couldn't face the party again. I had no idea what to do, but found that my feet had led me outside the house. It was cold, and my new coat, given in what I'd supposed was affection, was inside somewhere, secreted away by the phylarch's staff. I couldn't fetch it. I couldn't go back in there. But I wasn't completely sure of the way home. Some shred of sense surfaced in my mind and I found my way to the stable yard, which was full of carriages. I wasn't sure I'd recognise Malakess's among so many, but eventually I found a carriage that looked as if it was the one. Somehow I managed to ask the driver to take me home. I said I was unwell, which must have been patently obvious. Whether it was actually Malakess's driver or not, the har took sympathy on me and told me to hop inside. Hop was impossible; crawl, I could about manage.

I lay down on the plush bench and wept. Ridiculous clichéd thoughts such as 'how could he do this to me?' circled in my brain. Malakess knew my history. He couldn't and wouldn't do this, surely? I grieved for my newfound self as much as our potential relationship. Once again, I was Gesaril, soume shrew and predator, with enemies at his heels, wielding whips. But this time I was innocent. I'd done nothing deliberately. Was this the dehara's punishment for what I'd done to Jassenah? I'd been given the perfect life, only to have it snatched away, along with the heartless reminder of what I was. It was too cruel. As I lay there, wrung out, I remembered Haruah's words: don't make the same mistakes. I knew that. This was a chance to make amends to the universe. If Malakess really had deceived me, if what those snarling hara had said to me was true, I would walk away. I hadn't given Malakess my heart. It would be a sacrifice to lose him, but I could bear it. I must prove to myself and the world what I truly was. In that resolve lay strength. This was a test, nothing more, nothing less.

Huriel, as I've said before, had become like a parent to me, therefore his psychic antennae picked up my distress even before I entered the house. He was in hallway as I let myself in.

'Gesaril, you're back early,' he said, somewhat tensely.

I tried to keep my face averted. 'I feel ill,' I said.

'Ill? In what way?'

Part of me wanted to hug the night's events to myself in embarrassment, but another part was a harling who wanted to be comforted. I let Huriel see my face.

'By Aru, Gesaril, what's wrong?' he exclaimed, and came to take me in his arms.

That, of course, burst the banks of poisoned water inside me. My sobs were like retching. What had I been thinking? I was no sophisticated adult. Malakess would never weep like this over another har. I despised myself for doing it, even though I knew I wasn't just crying about Malakess. In fact, the other things were worse.

Huriel let the storm die down and then led me into the kitchen. I was relieved to note through blurred vision that Ystayne and Rayzie weren't there. Huriel pushed me into a chair by the wide old table and went into the larder. He returned with a bottle, sat down opposite me, poured two glasses of wine and pushed one towards me. I stared at it.

'Drink, then talk,' Huriel said.

I lifted the glass. It smelled of summer: some of Rayzie's rose petal wine. I drank, wept silently some more, then said, 'Huriel, I think I must go home.'

His eyes were very round. 'What?'

I held his gaze, but he clearly had no idea what was bothering me. I was tempted to open my mind to him, then thought better of it. 'Why didn't you tell me?'

He shrugged, almost irritably. 'Tell you what? What's going on?'

'About Malakess. About Iscane.'

I wanted him to ask again what I meant, but he dropped his eyes from mine. 'Oh,' he said.

'You knew,' I said, horrified. 'It's true, then. Malakess is chesna with his... *assistant.*'

Huriel screwed up his face, shook his head. 'Not chesna, no.' He sighed. 'Oh, Gesaril, there was nothing to tell, not really. Malakess and Iscane have lived together for years, but Malakess has never seen that as...' He shook his head again. 'This sounds bad, I know. I'm sorry.' He looked at me. 'What happened tonight?'

'A group of hara took it upon themselves to corner and threaten me with violence,' I said. 'They are friends of Iscane's.'

'That's preposterous,' Huriel said. 'What did Malakess say?'

'He doesn't know. I left the party.'

'But why?'

'Why?' A surge of anger went through me and I got to my feet. 'Why, Huriel? Do you really have to ask? You brought me here to get away from what happened in Jesith, to start again, but history is just repeating itself. The second generation hara here think the same of me as they did in Jesith. I'm a predator, a chesnari stealer! How could Malakess do this to me?'

'Hush,' Huriel said, making a placatory gesture with both hands. 'This is just a misunderstanding. Iscane can't have believed that he was chesna with Malakess. He's just staff.'

'Just staff? Like Rayzie and Ystayne are, here?' I snapped. 'Does that mean he's not a real har with feelings? He might only be *staff*, but that hasn't stopped Malakess from rooning him constantly for the past four years! In his position, I'd probably consider that a formal relationship too!'

'You must calm down,' Huriel said desperately. 'This can be sorted out.'

'No it *can't*,' I said. 'Hara's minds are made up. Those hara tonight knew about Ysobi and what happened. One of them told me he knew. I won't be this horrible thing they think I am, Huriel, I really won't. I don't want them to like me, but neither do I want them to despise me or mean me harm. I can't live here under that cloud. I've had enough of it. Why can't you see that? You know all about me.'

Huriel put his face in his hands for a moment, then raked his fingers through his hair. 'Look... Malakess sees you as different. It's not the same between you and him as it is between him and Iscane. He doesn't see Iscane as chesna material. It sounds blunt, but that's the truth of it. You know it yourself. These things happen all the time.'

'Do they?' I uttered a growl. 'I never knew that. Suddenly the Shadowvales seem incredibly attractive to me. Things like that didn't happen there. They didn't happen in Jesith, either.'

'He should have told you,' Huriel persisted bravely, 'and I have mentioned it to him. He didn't see it as important.'

'He'd have just cast Iscane out, moved me in?'

'No, of course not.'

I sat down again, put a hand to my face, rubbed hard. 'I can't believe he'd have moved me in there, into that situation. It would have been intolerable. Thank dehara I found out about this before that happened. But

113

it's still too late. I have a bad reputation here now as well.'

'That *will* be dealt with,' Huriel said firmly. 'You acted in all innocence.'

'No point,' I said. 'The only thing that will possibly change hara's minds is if I end it with Malakess, which is what I intend to do.'

'You can't!' Huriel exclaimed. 'Don't be ridiculous.'

'It's too late,' I said, 'way too late.' Picking up the wine bottle, I began to leave the room. I heard the scrape of Huriel's chair against the flagstones. 'Don't follow me,' I said, without looking round. 'I mean it, Huriel.'

He didn't.

Alone in my room, I drank from the bottle, fully intending and hoping that consuming the lot would render me unconscious. I didn't want to think. I didn't want to feel. I was incandescently furious one moment, inexpressibly miserable the next. That har tonight had looked at me with Jassenah's eyes, that same withering, curled lip contempt. I had sought to steal Ysobi away from Jassenah. I had meant to do it, and I hadn't cared. This was different. But hara wouldn't see it that way.

An hour or so later, I was lying on my back on the bed, rehearsing dozens of different scripts in my head, when I heard the sound of a carriage outside. It would be Malakess. The thought of seeing him made me feel nauseous. I couldn't face him tonight. Perhaps Huriel wouldn't think to come and ask me first. He might just send Malakess up to my room. I leapt from the bed, ran to the door, and turned the old key in the lock, then squatted on the floor with my face pressed to the wood. Sure enough, soon there were footsteps, but it was Huriel. He tried the door, made a sound of annoyance to find it barred to him. He knocked. 'Gesaril, open the door.'

'Go away,' I said.

'You must come down.'

'No. I won't see him tonight. He must leave.'

'Open the door,' he said, more softly. 'At least, talk to me.'

But the fact was, there was nothing to say. I'd already made up my mind. I had to take back control, and as far as I could see it, there was only one way to do that. I wanted to punish Malakess, yes, but I also wanted to be free of judgement. I wanted to make a gesture, show I wasn't bad. 'Tell him that if he wants to see me, he must come here tomorrow,' I said.

'This is unwise,' Huriel said. 'Talk to him now.'

'No. I'd say something I regret. I need some time.'

Huriel sighed. 'Very well. But I think you're making a mistake.' I heard his footsteps retreat.

Malakess turned up after lunch. I'd hardly slept, and had spent the night reconstructing defences around my heart. I went to him in the sitting room. He was standing in the middle of the floor. In his hands, he held my coat, which he offered to me. I didn't take it.

'Gesaril, I can quite understand your anger,' he said.

'I'm glad,' I replied.

'I have naturally removed Iscane from office,' he began, but before he could say more, I interrupted.

'What? You've fired him?'

'Of course. This is a regrettable situation. I will not have his friends threatening you like that. It's insupportable.'

'Iscane had nothing to do with it,' I said. 'You must reinstate him.'

'That's generous of you, but no. It's clear he must

go. I've already found him a position elsewhere.'

'Does he mean so little to you?' I asked, genuinely aghast. 'You'll just cast him aside like that and give him to somehar else? It's hypocritical of you, considering how you and Huriel criticised the Gelaming for suggesting you give me to the Nagini.'

'It's hardly the same,' Malakess said. 'Iscane has overstepped a mark. Whether he was anything to do with what happened last night or not, he has made huge assumptions and has led his friends to believe in them too. I never, at any time, indicated I considered our relationship to be chesna. His loose talk has embarrassed both you and me. Our feelings aside, that cannot go unpunished. I am High Codexia. I don't want scandal connected with my name.'

'Nor I!' I said angrily. I sighed. 'Look, the main issue here for me is what hara think of me in Kyme. I enjoy life here. I don't want it spoiled. I think it would be best for both of us if we ended our physical relationship.'

Malakess stared at me as if I'd spoken in a foreign tongue.

'I'm not being petty,' I said. 'I just don't want the hara here thinking badly of me. We've had some good times together, and we can still be friends and colleagues, but I won't be accused of wrecking other hara's lives. If I am with you, hara will always say I seduced and stole you from another har to advance my own position. I would rather advance my position through my own merit and preferably without making enemies.'

'You are quite happy just to end it?' Malakess snapped, as if he'd only heard half my words. 'Does our union mean nothing to you beyond the physical?'

'I consider you one of my dearest friends,' I said, 'but I'm not like other hara, Malakess. I have to protect myself and perhaps you too, in this case.'

'You haven't answered my question,' Malakess said.

'I think I have.'

'Yes,' he said softly, 'so you have.'

'I'll not forget what you've done for me. I hope we can remain friends.'

He inclined his head to me but said nothing. Before I could speak again, he left the room.

Huriel was so angry he couldn't bring himself to speak to me properly for two days. I felt as if I was made of ice. There were no emotions inside me. I went to my bed alone at night and lay awake, but I didn't mourn. I wouldn't let myself. I kept repeating over and over, *you didn't love him. It was nothing.* If Malakess's face came to my mind, I banished the image. I built a shell around myself, cold, unfeeling, mechanical. I didn't even let Huriel's behaviour affect me. I spoke to him as I always did and when he was curt with me, I made no comment.

Ystayne and Rayzie kept their distance, as if the toxic atmosphere in the house burned their skins. They retreated to the kitchens and stayed there, and I did not violate their territory. I went out into the town and kept my gaze straight ahead of me. I did my work for Huriel, but was not summoned to the library. I regretted that, but perhaps when this situation was old and stale, Malakess would call for me. I understood that he must be feeling embarrassed at the moment.

These last ten days have been really difficult. I haven't had the heart to write anything. I've just existed, tried almost to make myself invisible. I just want things to return to normal. Huriel and I have barely been speaking, but earlier today he said he wished to speak to me. From his tone, I gathered that this was not to be a friendly chat. We went to his office.

'You might like to know that Malakess is leaving Kyme,' he said.

'Where is he going?'

Huriel moved a few pens around his desk, not looking at me. 'To Immanion. This was discussed briefly while the Gelaming were here. Chrysm Luel thought it would be beneficial if a Sulh went to the Great Library in Immanion for some time. Malakess was in two minds, but given what's happened, he thought it would be best to go.'

I shrugged. *It's nothing to do with you*, I thought.

Huriel looked up and me shook his head. 'You've utterly confused me, Gesaril. You're not who I took you to be.'

'I don't know why you're so angry,' I said. 'If Malakess wasn't your friend, you'd feel differently. If I'd acted this way in Jesith, I wouldn't even be here now.'

Huriel pulled a sour face. 'How can you be so callous?'

'I'm not. Malakess had a relationship with somehar, but then thought I'd be a better prospect in terms of a consort. It all seems very political to me. I've stepped out of it. What's so bad about that?'

Huriel uttered a choked laugh. 'You think that was how he felt?' He sighed. 'Have I made you this monster? Is it my fault?'

I laughed. Perhaps I shouldn't have done. 'Monster? I'm trying to do the right thing. I wish I'd done it in Jesith. I'll not make the same mistake twice. There's no Huriel waiting for me this time, to take me away to a better life. I have to make my own.'

'It was just a few silly young hara,' Huriel said, punctuating his words with a stiff finger, he pointed at me. 'Just a few said some stupid things to you, and you deconstructed your entire future. Are you mad? Malakess loved you, Gesaril, but now he's castigating himself for giving his heart to so young a har. He's bereft, even if he can't show it.'

'He did not love me,' I said. 'He never said anything like that to me.'

'He wouldn't. But, that's probably for the best, since it's patently obvious you didn't feel the same. I'm not angry with you, just saddened.'

I rubbed my hands over my face. 'I'm saddened too, Huriel. I trusted Malakess. I really believed he was my future, but I can't be close to, never mind chesna, with a har who's so deceitful, and who would carelessly cast aside another, who's shared his bed for so long, just because he finds somehar he considers "better material". It's disgusting. You all wanted me to learn from what happened in Jesith, and I have. I agree it's probably best if Malakess leaves Kyme for a while. When he returns, all will be forgotten.'

'If he returns,' Huriel said. 'I can appreciate how you feel, I really can, but I think you're over-reacting.'

'I'm not. I had bruises to prove it, remember. I've thought about it all a lot and have tried to put Malakess in a positive light, but at the very least, he should have ended his association with Iscane before I started accompanying him to official events. There should have been some respectable gap. He should have told me everything from the start. I'd have been more careful.' I threw up my hands. 'Oh, I don't know. It's just a mess.' I appealed to Huriel with a wide-eyed gaze. 'I just want us to get back to how we were. I miss Malakess, and I'm really sorry I can't be with him, but try to understand how I feel. Please, Huriel! I can't live here with a horde of Jassenahs watching my every move.'

Huriel uttered a soft sound and drew me into his arms. I wanted to weep, but I couldn't. There was a hard painful lump in my throat, condensed emotion. 'I love you too,' Huriel said. 'You're like a son to me, Gesaril. Of course, we'll get back to how we were, but can't you at least go to Malakess, see him before he leaves?'

I pressed my face into Huriel's hair. 'Don't ask me to do that. Please.' The truth was, I didn't trust myself. If Malakess should do something like confess his feelings for me, I might well cave in and fall into his arms.

Huriel sighed. 'All right. I'll respect your decision, but it's just so sad, such a waste.'

Arahanisday, Adkayamoon 21

Today is the eve of Natalia and Kyme is infused with the spirit of this best of festivals. Snow lies thick upon the ground and every house is decorated with holly and ivy bows. The holly berries are shockingly red this year. Huriel says this is because we had a lot of rain. Tonight, we will attend a ritual and party at the Poltenemy manse, and then tomorrow some of Huriel's colleagues are coming over to spend the day with us. The house looks beautiful because Rayzie has decorated the ground floor throughout with evergreens and ribbons. The air smells of Natalia; an unmistakeable scent of cut greens, pine and spicy cooking that always has me thinking back to the days before my harlinghood was spoiled. Natalia is always a huge community party in the Shadowvales. Amazingly, I have received a gift from my parents accompanied by a letter from my hostling. They have sent me a vakei, a ritual blade. It really is beautiful, and I will use it always. My hostling congratulated me on my ascension to Brynie. I'd written to him to tell him about it. Who knows, one day we might actually become friends?

On to other matters… It appears that everyhar in Kyme has got to hear about the sorry tragedy of my affair with Malakess. I'm gratified to note that I'm regarded with a new kind of respect, because everyhar also knows that I've ended my relationship with the High Codexia. I'm not the soume shrew adventurer, after all. Not everyhar agrees with my decision, first generation particularly, but I gather from Ystayne and Rayzie that many pure borns consider that I've stood up for our generation, and have shown the haughty High Codexia that we're not to be used like bedroom toys. Now Malakess's house stands empty and snow drifts against the front door.

I do miss him terribly, but I'm glad that the hostility against me has died down. I've resolved never again to take aruna with anyhar unless I'm sure of their history. I look upon the whole episode as being like a rite of passage. If I have moments when my armour slips and I want to sit alone in a private place and grieve, I have more when I feel positive about myself and the future. In the new year, I'll begin work in the main library itself. A position has been offered to me, and it's not lost on me that the har who made the offer is second generation.

Of course, all this activity and scandal has meant I've had little time to be taken unawares by hauntings of earlier hurts. It's easier to push the sad ghosts away, shut the door on them, turn up the light.

Aloytsday, Snowmoon 2

Today, I had an unexpected visitor. Iscane turned up at the house, asking to see me. I'd heard he now worked for another Codexia but we'd not run into each other.

I met with Iscane in Huriel's office, a formal setting in which I felt most comfortable. Iscane looked healthy enough; there was no sign of despair or grief on his face. He's a very attractive har, clearly well educated and intelligent, and I honestly can't understand why Malakess should have considered me more worthy than him.

'I hope you don't mind me coming to see you,' Iscane said, and there was no longer iciness in his voice. His friendly mien made him appear more attractive. If he'd been like this with me from the start, if we'd become friends, then all the unpleasantness could have been avoided. I'd have never begun a relationship with Malakess, for a start.

'Not at all. What can I do for you?'

'Nothing,' he said, sitting down on a chair next to the fire. 'I just feel responsible for that episode at Poltenemy's party last Mistmoon. I keep thinking about it, so realised I really had to come and see you. New year, new starts... I want you to know I didn't ask Nasander and the others to act on my behalf. It was appalling behaviour.'

'Well, rightly or wrongly, you all had a set of beliefs about me,' I said. 'I can't say I was greatly pleased by what happened, but I'm also somewhat grateful for it. I really had no idea about you and Malakess.'

'I know,' Iscane said. 'Malakess told me.' He pulled a sad, sour face. 'He told me as he was kicking me out of my home.'

'I'm sorry about that,' I said. 'I did tell him he should reinstate you. I had no wish to cause you pain.'

'We were wrong about you,' Iscane said. 'Please accept my apologies on behalf of all of us.'

'You weren't wrong. I used to be the sort of har you thought I was. The fact is that what happened at the party helped me overcome my own past, and I'm grateful for that. So I accept your apology wholeheartedly.'

Iscane nodded. 'Then I hope we can all put it behind us. Would you have dinner with me this Aruhanisday? I would like to make amends.'

The thought of having to face the very group who'd confronted me left me cold, and I hesitated before answering. Iscane smiled, clearly having picked up on my reservations. 'Just you and I,' he said. 'Just dinner. I'd really like it if you'd accept.'

'Yes, thank you, I'd like that,' I said.

Iscane stood up. 'Good. I'll call for you about seven o'clock. I know you've not been out much in town since you arrived, so I'll take you to a good restaurant, show you around a bit.'

Pelfazzarsday, Snowmoon 6

And so, my formal introduction into the younger society of Kyme has commenced. Last night, Iscane took me to a place called Shivering Firs, which specialised in dishes from the Almagabran continent. He was charming and entertaining company, and more than once I found myself wondering why on earth Malakess hadn't been in love with him.

After two bottles of wine, and quite late into the evening, Iscane asked me teasingly, 'So, all that gossip about you was true? You had to be physically removed from Jesith to protect the reputation of the rooning Hienama?'

I laughed. 'Pretty much, yes. I had a crush on him, a really big one, and I behaved badly. He had a chesnari, and a new son. I don't know what possessed me.' A part of myself winced inside at these words. I didn't mean any of them, not really.

'Hmm, I've heard that Ysobi is quite something,' Iscane said. 'It was probably just a case of what we see so often; older hara taking advantage of us pure borns.'

I didn't think I was as political about it as all young hara in Kyme seemed to be. 'Not really,' I said. 'I knew what I was doing. Still, it's behind me now. I really appreciate you taking me out like this. I want to make my life here. I love Kyme.'

'I'll help you,' Iscane said. 'The har you'll be working with is a good sort. You can count on having a full social schedule, trust me!' He grinned. 'And if it's a chesnari you're looking for, we'll find you somehar deliciously appropriate.'

'Oh, I'm not looking for that,' I said. 'I just want to have a good time.'

'Good for you!'

Iscane lived in a converted stable in the grounds of his new employer. He enthused about this place, and how much better it was than Malakess's house, which he considered 'draughty'. 'I'm much happier now,' he said. 'Looking back, it's easy to see how miserable I was without even realising it. I spent the entire time waiting for Malakess to give me attention. Isn't it odd, the way that once it's all over, and the emotions have gone, you can't believe the way you felt?'

A freezing wave went through me. There it was; a whisper in the room, a cold spot, a ghost. 'Yes, it's odd,' I said. 'It's such a breakthrough when you think of him, and then realise it's the first time you've thought of him for days, when before he was on your mind all the time.'

'That's exactly it!' Iscane said. I could tell he thought we were both talking about Malakess.

'Do you miss him?' Iscane asked.

I paused. 'I'll never forget him. It just wasn't meant to be. But he helped me a lot. And his chesnari helped me too.'

Iscane coloured a little and smiled at the table. 'It's his pleasure.' I felt the pressure of a foot against my right leg. He'd taken off his shoes, and his long bare toes flexed against me. My flesh contracted. It felt as if a sleeping snake stirred drowsily in my belly. *Why not?* I thought. This would be uncomplicated, and it was something I'd have to do eventually. 'I'd like to see your new home,' I said.

'I'd like to show it to you,' Iscane responded. 'We could go there now, if you want.'

'I want.'

He laughed. 'Let me pay the bill. Won't be long.'

I watched him slink across the restaurant, a tall, slim perfect har, his long fair hair swinging loose down his back.

We walked back arm in arm, kicking up the powdery snow. Iscane wore a huge fur coat and at one point he stopped walking and enveloped me into its musky warmth. We shared breath, snowflakes settling on our hair and clothes. 'You taste like roses,' Iscane murmured.

'And you like honey,' I said.

'What a tasty combination.' He put his lips to mine once more.

Iscane's apartment was on the first floor of the old building and to reach it we had to climb some very narrow stairs that creaked ominously. The space above was one huge room, and was indeed a very tasteful and comfortable place. A huge fire burned in a wide hearth, well stocked with logs. I wondered whether Iscane had planned on bringing me here all along, seeing as the room was so nicely warmed. His bed lay beneath a skylight in the arched ceiling. There were many furs upon it. 'Get undressed,' Iscane said. 'I want to see you naked. I'll get us something to drink.'

He went over to the far side of the room, while I pulled off my clothes. I stretched out on the furs, aflame with anticipation. Iscane came back to me and handed me a tall glass of red wine. He stared at me in appreciation. 'It seems almost pointless to say it, but you're lovely,' he said.

'So are you.'

He smiled. 'Wait, you've not seen everything yet.'

He gave me a show, disrobing slowly and sensuously. One of his nipples was pierced with a silver ring. He turned his back on me to ease off his trousers, displayed his perfect buttocks to me. I wanted to bite him. Then he turned around and I saw he wanted to be ouana. He was larger than Malakess and a tremor of uncertainty went through me.

'Iscane,' I said.

He came to the bed, straddled my prone body and pushed his hair back over his shoulders. 'What?' He leaned down to nibble my chest.

'Be careful with me.'

He laughed. 'Roon, of course. But what do you mean?'

'I've had problems with soume, a childhood injury.'

He frowned. 'Oh, poor you. Would you like to be ouana?'

'No, just... take care.'

'Direct me,' he said. 'We'll take it slow.'

And slow it was, almost too slow. He had me writhing beneath him with need, yelling out his name. I felt stretched, but not torn. The slight ache was actually delicious. At the end, he allowed himself to be more forceful; it was intoxicating. Aruna with Ysobi, I realised, had never been like this. I'd been obsessed with him as a har, but my problems had been too great for aruna to be anywhere near what it should have been. And with Malakess, I'd still been getting over Ysobi. Our aruna life had been decorous in comparison to the free abandon characterised by Iscane. He and I felt more like equals, and there was a lack of reserve and inhibition in him that made things easy for me.

'Doesn't seem to be anything wrong with *you!*' Iscane declared.

'Don't stop. No, there's nothing wrong. Iscane, don't stop.'

'I'm yours for as long as I can maintain a stalk,' he said, which sounded incredibly funny to me at the time. I was still laughing when the next peak came, but almost delirious by the final wave.

Afterwards, we lay side by side, drinking the wine and talking. I knew that probably within only a few hours, all of Iscane's friends would hear about what had happened. I hoped he would deliver a good report.

'Have you ever gone double flower?' Iscane asked me.

'No, what's that?'

'You haven't?' He laughed. 'Wonderful. Wait till you see.'

'But what is it?'

'Pike mouth first.'

'What?'

'Pike mouth, you know? On each other?'

'No...'

He sighed, but was smiling. 'Hmm, seems I have a lot to teach you. This is pike mouth.' He leaned over me and took my ouana-lim between his lips.

'Oh, *that*. Yes, I know what you mean.'

'OK, we do it to each other.'

He manoeuvred himself so this was possible. This was something I'd never done before, and it was as if we were one creature, a serpent eating its own tail, but that was not the treat he wanted to share. It was just the preliminary. Once we were both high on aruna, Iscane pushed me onto my back and slowly lowered himself onto my ouana-lim. 'Use your hands on me,' he said, guiding my fingers to his flowering ouana-lim. After that, he did most of the work. Ouana and soume at the same time. I hadn't believed such a thing was possible. When his soume-lam contracted to meet my peak, aren also jetted out of him and he uttered a shout that sounded like a cry of pain. His soume-lam gripped me like a metal fist. I was showered in his glowing fluid, and I'm sure it encouraged my own flow. I seemed to peak for longer than usual.

'That is double flower,' he said, still panting upon me. His hair was dark with sweat. 'And before you ask, yes it does hurt a bit, like a needle through the groin but it's a pain you want again and again. Want to try?'

'Well... yes... but now? Already?'

Iscane laughed. 'You've spent far too much time with first gen. Welcome to the world of youth. Flowering again post peak makes it even more powerful. It just takes a little longer.'

And so it did. We were soft in each other's mouths for a while, but I felt extremely tingly and when the hardness happened it was sudden and almost brutal. Iscane guided me onto him and took my ouana-lim in his hands. It was the most strange sensation, and not altogether pleasant. The ouana-lim's instinct is to retract into the body when soume is stimulated, but when it's aroused, it can't do that. It's impossible to describe exactly what it feels like but it kindles a need that you are sure can never be satisfied. A peak with a distinctly different flavour built inside me, and when it cascaded through me, so my ouana-lim synchronised and experienced its own release. Iscane was right. It hurt as if my body was being cut in two. But it was the most powerful physical sensation imaginable.

'Did you like that?' Iscane asked me.

'I'm not sure *like* is the right word,' I said. 'It's... well... I see what you mean.'

'With three or more hara, you can imagine what can be achieved,' Iscane said. 'But that's a treat we must save for another time. Let's have another drink. Before we sleep, I want you to roon me senseless, in single flower. There are a few more tricks I can teach you to make me lose my mind with pleasure. Can you keep up?'

I laughed. 'Your stamina is pretty amazing, but I

think I can just about survive.'

'Good.' He pushed me off him. 'Move over. I need to open another bottle.'

This morning, I awoke before Iscane did. He was lying on his belly beside me, one arm cast across my chest. Gently, I eased myself from under him, and rose from the bed. I went to his kitchen area to get myself a drink of water. Unaccountably, I felt depressed. As I sat drinking the icy water, gazing out of the yard below, I remembered a dream I'd had. In it, I'd been taking aruna with Iscane, soume beneath him. Then I'd seen movement in the shadows beyond the bed and saw that Malakess was standing there, his face grey and constricted with grief. I was overcome with shame and remorse, and then it was Malakess upon me, deep inside me. 'I loved you,' he said. 'And you have forgotten me already.' And then it was Ysobi above me. 'You won't forget,' he said. 'Not ever. I *am* you.'

I couldn't remember any more of the dream. Perhaps that had been it. The fact was, I now felt strangely guilty even though I knew I'd done nothing wrong. Iscane was a free young har, as was I. Malakess had left Kyme. There was no reason why Iscane and I shouldn't be intimate. It was part of life. Yet still that sad dream ghost haunted my mind. My heart ached with longing, but it wasn't for Malakess. *I loved you... so much.* As I stared out of the window at the snow covered land, I was suffused with a memory of Jesith; the smell of the place, the ambience. I was filled with a sense of Ysobi, as if he stood towering behind me. When he'd held me, my face would always rest against his chest. I'd listened to his heart beat. Then it all came back to me in a powerful rush. The coldest wave.

The night I told him how I felt.

I think he already knew, of course he did, but I knew that if I didn't speak my heart I would literally explode. I'd sat before his chair on the floor. He held on to my hands as I spilled it all. He stroked me with his thumbs, and he looked at me with such tenderness, hardly even blinking, for what must have been over an hour. That was the worst aspect. If he'd been indifferent, or just concerned in a teacherly sort of way, it might have been easier. But that look. No har had ever looked at me like that before, and I doubt they will again. Within his eyes was this unspoken *thing*. Such tenderness. There is no other way to describe it. When there was nothing more to say, he'd pulled me close and I'd got to my knees to rest my chin on his shoulder. 'I am here for you,' he'd said, but not in the way I wanted. 'I will always be here.'

But of course, he wasn't.

As I recalled that night, which I had tried to bury so thoroughly, I began to weep; those gut deep choking sobs that are the end of all hope. Every har in Jesith believed I was a scheming fool. They hadn't been there. They hadn't seen. Sometimes I'd doubted my own sanity, because I remembered that night so clearly, yet it was as if I'd only dreamed it. When things had got too messy, Ysobi had made the decision to abandon me. I think that hurts me more than the fact he didn't want me. He hung me out to dry. How could I ever forgive that?

Now that I'd let these feelings out, they wouldn't stop flowing. I couldn't stop weeping. I didn't want Iscane to see me like this, and even if I managed to pull myself together, I had no doubt that the psychic reverberations of the aruna we'd shared would mean he'd intuit my every feeling for next day or so. Somehow, taking deep breaths, I got control of myself. Leaving Iscane a note to thank him, but claiming I needed to be back at Huriel's for a lunch engagement, I left his apartment.

Outside the world was blindingly white and untouched. A few harlings were out playing in the pristine snow, and in a field nearby three young horses galloped through it, drunk on life.

Lunilsday, Frostmoon 25

In just a couple of short months my life has changed so much it's as if I've woken up in a different universe. My supervisor at the Library, an under Codexia named Crytah, is, as Iscane predicted, responsible for me hardly ever having a moment to myself, in both a working and social sense. I now have dozens of friends, and many of them I know intimately. Aruna is as much a part of socialising with these hara as sharing a meal. Life is a dizzying whirl and I am caught up in it, and yet some part of me isn't there, not really. I feel like I'm faking it. Fortunately nohar seems to notice this, but then the young hara of Kyme – or at least those associated with the Academy and Library – don't appear to pay much attention to the more serious aspects of life. My first impressions of fusty academics were misplaced. While the older hara might be like that, the second generation hara aren't. They are hedonistic and carefree at night, yet able to work hard during the day. Their openness about aruna, and their fascination with experimenting is not only educational but liberating. It's difficult to feel inhibited around them, because despite their lustful behaviour they are in another way very innocent. Their frankness and wonder has charm. And they think I'm one of them, but I'm not. It seems that even as I grow, becoming more established in Kymian society, I am in some ways becoming more estranged from it. Perhaps I am really going mad and splitting into two people in my head.

As to what I am, I still don't know. I find myself thinking of Ysobi and then Malakess quite a lot despite my aggressive attempts at exorcism. Huriel and I are working on my next level of training – Acantha, the first tier of Ulani. The strange thing is that as I learn to observe myself more, I feel I know less about myself. Knowledge is a strange thing. The more you have of it, the less you seem to know. Huriel says this is normal, part of my development. He occasionally gets letters from Malakess but I've not received one. I don't suppose I should expect to, even though I didn't want us to become so estranged. So many times I've thought of writing to him, but something stops me.

I sent another present to Jassenah, just some trinkets I picked up, and a short while later I received a letter from him. The same stuff as before; news of everyone in Jesith but for Ysobi. The hot pain I used to feel has subsided since that morning in Iscane's apartment, but there is still... something. Sometimes I wake up in the night from a dream of him, and my heart is pounding as if I've been running. Then I wonder whether he's dreamed of me too. Often I speak his name aloud, which seems like a magical and potent thing to do. But this is all mixed up in confusing feelings about Malakess. Did I really care about him or was he just a substitute? I can't speak to anyhar about this, so I have to work it out on my own. Winter is still all around us, but its grip is breaking. I like the spring. It's a turning time, when anything seems possible. I hope it will bring me something good.

Aruhanisday, Windmoon 7

Yesterday was the anniversary of the day I woke up to a new feeling. I'll always remember it. I just looked at Ysobi that day and saw him differently. It is the moment when you look upon a har and think that you will know him for the rest of your life. I gazed at Ysobi and saw a fountain. I realised that the uplifting feelings I'd been experiencing over the past weeks had been the touch of his energy against my own. He was nourishment to me. Suddenly, as if a veil had been lifted, I saw this incredibly deep beauty in him, and it was shocking. A wave of cold and heat went through me; I did in truth behold a different har before me. I looked at him and thought, 'is this what love feels like?' And he looked at me too, threw back his head very slightly in a sort of theatrical gesture, as if he too had just had a revelation about something. He smiled in that enigmatic way he has, eyes ablaze. We said nothing to one another, but afterwards it felt as if we'd talked for hours.

The universe rolls and turns. It positions challenges and trials, perhaps even demons, in our path, that lie in wait for us. I don't know what is going to happen to me from this point forward, but I must relate what has led to this moment.

I asked Crytah for the day off from work, because I wanted time alone. The thought of other haras' voices was intolerable. I needed the quiet of nature around me. It wasn't that I wanted to dwell and brood upon the past, but in my mind, I did need to visit a grave and place a flower upon it.

It was a perfect morning. The sky looked as if the dehara had painted it several times to get that intense and faultless hue. It had rained before the dawn, so the land seemed to be drying out after a protracted session of weeping. There was a freshness to the air that smelled of purged sadness to me. Even as I ate my breakfast, I was eager to immerse myself in the landscape. It called to me with a lilting song that I could almost hear with my physical ears. The song of life. Huriel was chatting away amiably, but I don't think I heard half of what he said.

When I went outside, I could sense the change in the air. It was as if the earth had rolled over in its sleep, and had uttered a waking sigh. I walked over the old bridge, which is covered in moss. Below it lies a straight road, overgrown with grass that somehar had once told me humans used for vehicles that ran on tracks. Most of the tracks have gone, because they have been used for building. Spring flowers were beginning to unfurl. The air tasted green.

And it was down in the meadows that I saw him. He was like a spirit, an emanation of the world itself, perhaps of the season, walking slowly through the woken grass. I knew at once he was of the Nagini, simply because of his clothes and the colour of his skin. His hair was loose down his back like a banner and it seemed to me as if tiny flowers fell from his skin as he walked. In such a way is beauty recognised. I knew at once this sighting was important and relevant. A dehar had come to me, and I followed him.

He went to the old pools, where the gentle cattle came to drink, and here the naked whips of the willows dipped into the dark waters. He knew I was watching him, of course, because no matter how fey and distant he appeared, I became aware of his own awareness.

As I stood among the willows behind him he spoke,

and at first I thought it was in my head. He said, 'I will send a dream to you.' And then I somehow came to my senses, half dazed, and found myself alone.

I fell asleep among the early flowers, and there dreamed of a mighty city surrounded by green fields. At the edge of one of the fields was a deep ravine and when I looked into it, I expected to see a horse, but what I saw instead was a lion. It looked up and caught my eye and I could see at once it was fierce and hungry. My companion, for I had one suddenly, even though I could not see them exactly, exclaimed how beautiful this creature was and went to the edge of the ravine to reach down toward it. I cried out in alarm and told my friend to draw back, that the creature was angry and would attack us. I saw that indeed the lion was now leaping up to try and escape its prison, and as I looked upon it, so other creatures manifested around it, pure white tigers, snarling and twisting and reaching up with their great paws.

'But how beautiful they are,' said my friend and knelt at the edge of the ravine reaching down. I could not pass the obstruction of this wayward friend, and the tigers were leaping ever closer to the edge, swiping with their claws, clearly intent on blood. Then, just as one of the tigers nearly scrambled onto the field, my friend appeared to realise our predicament and cried 'Run!'

And so we ran, and behind us came the velvet pound of relentless paws. We ran into the city and the tigers followed us. There seemed so many of them now, and they were all of different colours, but it was the white tigers that caught my attention. They threw themselves into the air and spun round to become invisible. They plunged and pounced and all around them hara were running and screaming.

I had brought the tigers into the city. It would never

be free of them again.

When I woke from this dream, I felt strangely revitalized, and it was as well I felt that way. As I walked back to the house, I was asking the universe, show me what I must do. There is a feeling inside me. I'm not sure what it is, but it's something.

Huriel was flustered in the library. 'I know you've got a day off, but will you go up to the academy for me? Abraxxas wanted these notes, and I would go myself, but I have all this to do.' He indicated a mess of papers on his desk.

'No problem,' I said and bent to kiss the top of Huriel's head.

He glanced up at me, his expression bemused. 'What's wrong with you?'

'Nothing. The air is just good today.'

He smiled. 'Good. I've been concerned about you lately. You've seemed distant. Perfectly normal and yet distant. I've sensed it.'

'I'm fine. Give me the notes.'

'Are you going out tonight?'

'I don't know yet. Don't fuss.'

I considered having some lunch first, then thought, well, I won't be that long, and opted for getting the little task out of the way first. Actually, I wasn't that hungry.

The academy was very busy, hara milling about the entrance hall. What event was going on? I couldn't recall that one was scheduled. I began to push my way through the crowd, intent on reaching Abraxxas's office as quickly as possible. I was concerned somehar would spot me and ask me to do another job. As I reached the main staircase, my steps faltered. Every single har in the room faded to a blur, but for one. He stood with his back to me. Very tall, a flag of burnished hair. Malakess. I knew him even from behind. Nohar had told me he was coming back. Still, with my centred mood, I was more than capable of dealing with this situation. I composed myself for a cheerful greeting.

As I reached out to touch his arm, I said, 'Kess, how are you?'

He turned then and we stared at one another. I thought, *you look like him more than ever. This is cruel.* I must have just looked stunned.

'Gesaril,' he said. 'This is a... surprise.'

It wasn't Malakess. How could I have thought it was? 'Ysobi,' I managed to say. 'I'm sorry... I thought you were...'

'Dead?' he said and laughed.

'No, I thought you were Malakess. What are you doing here?' It was surprisingly easy to talk. I felt calm. Why should that be?

'I was asked to come,' he said. 'A conference of hienamas, a conclave.' He grimaced. 'Sinnar felt I should come.'

'How is everyhar in Jesith?' I enquired.

He nodded his head slowly a couple of times. 'Fine. Life is as it always is. You know Jesith.'

I winced a bit. In his position, I would not have said that. 'Good. Well... I'd better get on.' I waved the packet I was carrying. 'I have work to do.'

'You look well,' he said. 'Life here clearly suits you. I'm glad.'

Don't say any more, I thought. I managed a smile. 'Yes, I like it here. Anyway...'

'We should catch up,' he said. 'Tell me about what you've been doing.'

'Er... yes... maybe.'

He put his head to one side. 'Gesaril, we should.

There shouldn't be awkwardness between us.'

How he could say that astounded me. I was actually shocked into speechlessness for some moments. There were so many snarling retorts I could make to that suggestion, that he really deserved, but all I said was, 'If that's what you want.'

'It is,' he said, and smiled. 'I had a feeling I'd run into you today. I'm really pleased to see you so well. All I ever wanted was for you to be happy.'

And all I ever wanted was you. His fond concern was like poison to me, because it wasn't the sort of fondness I craved. How could he expect me to sit somewhere making small talk with him? There would be so many things I couldn't say; it would be torture. 'Are you here for long, then?'

'About a week, maybe.' He shrugged. 'I'll have to see how it goes.'

'Oh.'

He gave me an inscrutable look, long enough for me to lower my eyes from it. 'Jass will get annoyed with me if I'm away for too long.'

As ever, the surgeon's precision with a remark that would cut. 'I'm sure. Well, I really must be…'

He took hold of my arm to stop me leaving. 'I'll be free later. How about dinner? You can take me somewhere interesting.'

A voice inside me was screaming: *Don't do it! Don't do it!* Naturally, I ignored it. 'OK. Where are you staying?'

'The Ivy House in the grounds here. A few of us are there.'

'Will eight o'clock be all right? I can call for you.'

'Perfect,' he said. 'See you later, then.'

'See you later.'

Somehow, on legs that felt as if they were made of

141

paper, I got up the stairs, turned into the first corridor and there, leaned against the wall. I fanned myself with the notes package. I put one hand over my mouth. I laughed. Then there were tears in my eyes. *Are you insane?* My inner voice demanded. *You really shouldn't do this. You know you shouldn't.*

'Oh shut up!' I said aloud, and went to deliver Huriel's package.

As you can imagine, I have been thrown into in a completely peculiar state of mind. Part of me is filled with anger and a great desire to inflict some kind of revenge on Ysobi, another part is ecstatic at the prospect of seeing him again, and yet another part is terrified.

When I returned home from my errand, I had no intention of saying anything to Huriel, sure of his disapproving response, but, like the fussing surrogate parent he has become, he noticed something was afoot the minute I stepped back inside the house. I suppose I brought it with me, the spectre of my impending assignation, like a large roaring fire that curled the wallpaper from the very walls and made it too hot to walk upon the floors.

'Gesaril!' Huriel called, emerging from his office. 'Did you deliver my package?'

'Of course I did,' I replied lightly, making great effort to appear and feel – to Huriel's senses – normal.

Huriel narrowed his eyes. 'What's happened?'

This was a crucial moment. I could lie, which would inevitably be found out, and would perhaps damage my relationship with Huriel, or I could tell the truth and get a lecture. 'Well...'

Huriel folded his arms. He meant business. 'Gesaril, there's no point trying to hide anything from me. What is it you have to tell me?'

'You'll be angry,' I said, sighing.

'Then tell me quickly to get it over with.'

'Ysobi is here in Kyme.' I held my breath.

'What? Why?'

'He said he was summoned…'

'You've *seen* him? Spoken to him?'

'Yes.'

Huriel frowned and when he spoke it was as if to himself, not me. 'I know nothing about any summons, and I surely would have done. He hasn't contacted me.'

'*Does* he contact you?'

Huriel glanced at me. 'Of course. We are friends. I am his mentor.'

'You've never told me this before. Has he spoken to you about me?'

Huriel didn't appear to hear my question. 'He said he would never come here. I told him not to…'

'Huriel!' I took a few steps towards him. 'You've spoken to Ysobi about me… recently?'

Huriel sighed. 'I was never going to tell you but… yes. Not that recently. I thought it was in your best interest after you confided in me that day.'

'How can I ever trust you?' I snapped. 'First the secrecy about Malakess, now this. You disappoint me… greatly.'

Huriel pulled a despairing face. 'It was because I cared about you that I kept silent. Also, you have to face the reality that I've known Ysobi for a long time. Much as it might gall me, I have to respect his privacy too.'

He might as well have been standing there punching me in the face. I was so angry, I felt oddly calm. 'So what was the content of your discussions? You might as well tell me now.'

'It's irrelevant. What I want to know is what he's doing here.'

'I don't think it's irrelevant. Tell me.'

Huriel put his hands upon my arms. I wanted to lash out and throw him off but remained stiff and unyielding in his hold. 'You know that I love you. You are like family to me and I don't want to see you hurt. Ag knows what Ysobi's doing here, but it's vital you don't look on it as a sign of hope. You do understand that, don't you?'

'Utterly. I'm meeting him for dinner later.'

Huriel actually shook me. 'No, you are not! Don't even think about it.'

'He asked me to.'

'Stay away!' Huriel insisted. 'Don't go near him. Please.'

'It's only dinner,' I said. 'Why make such a fuss? He's here because of official hienama business. We ran into each other, we made an arrangement to share a meal. That's hardly high drama.'

Again Huriel sighed. He would not let me go. 'Gesaril...' He held his breath, clearly debating with himself. 'Look... I asked him outright, a long time ago. I asked him how it was between you. He had no reason to lie to me, and even through correspondence and ether communication, I would be able to tell if he was lying. He told me he felt nothing for you. He told me you'd... well, not made it up exactly, but that you'd totally misinterpreted his behaviour.'

Now I did throw him off. I felt stunned. 'You believed him? You thought I was a liar, even after I told you everything?'

'No, I didn't think you were a liar.'

'So you humoured me. You indulged my deluded little fantasy. You said nothing. How could you do that?'

Huriel at least had the grace to look ashamed of himself. 'I just thought it was the worst case of crossed wires I'd ever come across.'

'What does that mean?'

'It means that you wanted to see something there, and the way Ysobi is with everyhar... well, you read too much into it.'

'I... what?' I put my hands to my face, so angry with Huriel it made my eyes ache. All this time, he'd let me believe he sympathized with me, while he'd privately thought I was out of my mind.

'I'm astonished he's here,' Huriel said, 'which is why I have to tell you this. We'd already agreed he'd keep a distance, even though he used to visit here quite regularly. I'm cross with him that he's come, especially since he's not told me about it in advance. I don't know what he's playing at, or why he's made contact with you like this. But it's not good, and you must stay away. All that will happen is that it will hurt you more. He's no good for you, Gesaril. He doesn't care. Harsh as that sounds, keep it in the forefront of your mind. He has his life and he's content with it. You have no place in it.'

'Is it really so astonishing he wants to see me?' I said. 'Am I that repellent?'

'Don't be ridiculous. Of course he finds you attractive. Who wouldn't? But he has no intention of doing anything about it. He doesn't feel the same as you do. To do this now is just cruel. I'm very disappointed in him.'

'Disappointment all round, it seems.'

'Are you still going to see him later?'

'Yes.'

'I broke a vow, telling you what I did,' Huriel said. 'I can see how angry you are with me, but please think of my position in all this. I can see from your face that nothing I say will change your mind. All I ask is that you do not reveal what you know. And be careful. I have told you the truth as I've been told it.'

'He made you vow not to tell me he didn't give a damn?' I asked icily.

'Essentially... yes.'

'I see. What puzzles me then is, if he really cares so little, why it should bother him if I know that glorious little truth?'

I didn't wait for Huriel's response. I walked away. He didn't call me back.

Now I am in my room, writing. What's going to happen to me? Who can I trust? Certainly not myself, and certainly not Huriel. The way my body feels, full of swirling energy, the way my heart feels, it's as if I've just slipped back in time a year. Has Ysobi asked to eat with me simply to be friends? But he knows the way I feel. Why is he here, really? This is so dangerous; I know it is. Ysobi made me ill, yet here I am exposing myself to the infection again. I can't keep away.

Pelfazzarsday, Windmoon 9

I suppose it was anger more than anything that stood at my shoulder as I walked towards The Ivy House last night. As to who I was most angry with, I could not tell. I'd been made to feel like a monster and yet part of me knew – and had always known – that none of it would have happened if Ysobi had not been a conspirator. When I'd first met him I'd thought he was a freak, and a rather tedious one at that, but it had been both his warmth and his personality that had eventually made me see him differently. Sometimes, I had ached for him because he'd had such a vulnerable quality. At those times, the bands about my heart had drawn tighter; it had made me love him more. So many times over the past year, I'd doubted my memory, as if the things he'd said to me, the way he'd been with me, hadn't happened at all, and it really was all in my imagination. Strangely enough, it had been Huriel who'd helped me keep a grip on my sanity, and now I'd discovered that that too was a lie. For a moment, as I walked through the dark, with the scent of evening all around me, I saw the triviality of it all. I faltered on the path. What was the point of this meeting? Nothing good could come of it. Even if Ysobi was playing games and I ended up in his bed, no doubt the following morning he'd deny it happened or else say it was all my doing. And I would be left to cope with the aftermath. Again.

Turn back... The voice of my heart was most insistent. I must. I really must. This was a nexus point. If I turned away now, if I refused to see him, avoided him even, he would go away and leave me alone.

But then there was another voice; a voice I could not hear with my physical ears. *You cannot run away from it.* There were no words in my head; just a touch, just a wisp of feeling. I shivered and turned round.

And there on the path before me was a ghost of the twilight. I stared at it until it swam into focus from the distance, and I saw that it was my Nagini spirit from the water meadows. He was dressed in some pale, floating garment, with a scarf around his head, the tassels of it dangling down. I opened my mouth to utter a greeting, for surely we knew one another, but he put a finger to his lips. In mind touch, he said to me: *don't stray from the path, even if it is hard. You must follow it...*

I couldn't organize my thoughts to compose a response. I simply watched him walk past me until he faded into the darkness once more. I stared at the place where he had vanished for some moments and then I continued to walk to The Ivy House. Some destinies cannot and must not be avoided.

I took Ysobi to the restaurant where Iscane had taken me that first time. There were hara there I knew, who were clearly interested in my companion. I made a few cursory introductions as we walked between the tables, all the time thinking: *he is with me. He is walking behind me. It's really happening.* But it didn't feel real. It could have been anyhar behind me.

We sat down, and Ysobi said, 'This is rather... upmarket, Gesaril. Is this the sort of place where you spend your time?'

'Upmarket?' I frowned at him. It was obvious what it meant, but I pretended ignorance because it was an ancient term.

Ysobi rolled his eyes. 'OK, it seems... a place for high ranking cliques. You never struck me as a har who'd be into such things.'

I shrugged. 'My friends come here.' I signalled to the waiter, who glided to our table as if he floated some inches above the ground. 'Shall I order for both of us?' I asked.

Ysobi smiled at me inscrutably, his eyes were blue flames. 'As you wish.'

I must admit it made me feel good to speak with confidence to the waiter. I felt sophisticated and in control, conscious all the while of Ysobi's somewhat humorous gaze upon me.

The order attended to, I folded my hands upon the table. 'So, what brings you to Kyme exactly?'

'As I said, a meeting of hienamas,' Ysobi replied. 'We need more organization, training facilities.'

I laughed. I couldn't help it. 'By Aru, could the students keep up with you?'

He bridled a little at that. 'It's important that hara achieve their full potential. Too many neglect themselves in a spiritual and psychic sense. It's not deliberate, just a product of hara who were once human producing harlings and subconsciously passing on their own upbringing. You must know what I mean.'

It took all of my will not to react badly. 'I see the sense of it, yes. But part of me can't help feeling it's telling hara what's good for them, rather than letting them find out for themselves.'

'You were never good with authority, were you?' Ysobi observed.

The waiter returned with our wine and we were silent as he poured it for us. I sensed ice in the atmosphere between Ysobi and I; sparring words, a certain viciousness.

'So what have you been doing with yourself here in Kyme?' Ysobi asked, once the waiter had retreated once

149

more.

'Working for Huriel,' I said. 'I live in his house.'

Ysobi nodded. 'I know that.'

'I know you know.' I wanted to say more but reined myself in. 'It's been very… educational.'

'I'm sure.'

I wondered if Huriel had ever told Ysobi about Malakess and me. Surely not. 'It's better for me than the Shadowvales, in any case. I won't be going home. Well, this is my home now.'

'You've obviously fitted in really well. You were meant to come.'

'Perhaps,' I said, then couldn't resist adding, 'but perhaps not in the way it happened.'

Ysobi stared at me, and somehow I managed to hold his penetrating gaze. 'Do you want to talk about it?' he asked. 'I'm fine with that, if you do.'

Could you get any more arrogant? I thought. With effort, I managed a smile. 'I think I said everything that possibly could be said. What's the point? You made yourself perfectly clear to me.' *Or rather, to others.* But of course I couldn't say that.

'I'm sorry,' he said. 'I'm really sorry you got hurt. It wasn't my intention. I had no idea.'

You opened me up like a corpse on a slab, I thought. *You laid me bare, and gave to me such strength and warmth. Then you denied all that and made it out to be something else. How can I sit here and talk with you about it, when you refuse to admit you were part of it?*

'There's nothing else to say,' I said.

'You don't know how much I've wracked myself over what happened…'

I wished he'd stop. I didn't want to hear it.

'It made me look at myself in a different way… I realised there had to be changes in the way I interacted with my students.'

And now another har reaps the benefit of it.

Mercifully, our food arrived, not that I felt like eating. In fact, I wanted to leave. So close, yet so far, a table top away, and a host of self delusions in between. We sat in silence, playing with the meal. This wasn't working at all. Yet how to escape with dignity?

'Why are you here?' I asked him.

'You know,' he replied, not looking up from his food. 'A meeting…'

'I meant here, now. Why?'

He looked at me then. 'I want us to be friends.'

'Ah, you mean tidy the past away so you can feel comfortable about it?'

He grimaced. 'That is not what I meant. Don't twist my words.'

'Twist them? That would be hard. They're twisted enough.'

'No they're not. That is the truth.'

'Well, I wouldn't want to be friends with me.'

He was beginning to acquire the dark expression of anger that presages those bursts that occasionally flare out of him. I know he hates that about himself, but he clearly couldn't help it. 'Don't put yourself down…'

'I'm not. What I meant was if some har had said to me, and been with me, in the way I was with you, and I felt nothing for him, I'd run from him like a frightened horse. Yet here you are. You know how I feel, Ysobi. Why sit here and talk about being friends? You're not stupid, so you must know that's an impossible request.'

'I thought that time might have healed you,' he said. 'I thought you might have forgotten some of it.'

I laughed sourly. 'You're the hienama, not me. Surely you're wise enough to know that a year is not enough to get over what happened between us. For your information, the love I experienced could not simply be taken down and packed away like Natalia decorations.'

'I was never worth it,' he said. How he'd always loved to say that. He'd never meant a word of it either. It had been his convenient escape.

I put down my knife and fork very carefully. I took a deep breath. Then I made a signal to the waiter. When he came to my side, I asked for the bill. Ysobi just stared at me. 'What are you doing?' he asked.

'You can see,' I replied. 'I won't play this charade, Yz. I can't do it. I'm going. By all means stay and finish your meal. You might like to think about why you're actually here while you're doing so. But I'm not playing your game. I won't make you feel better. So here it is: I still love you and always will. I believe you felt something for me but chose to smother it and make me the scapegoat for it all. Now, it is grotesque sitting here talking with you and I want to leave.' I stood up and put some money on the table. 'I hope your meeting goes well.'

Up behind the town there is a place where grey rocks poke out from a hillside over a valley below. After I left the restaurant, I climbed to this place, my mind and heart numb. I sat down on the cool grey stone that seemed to hang in space, not attached to the earth. I stared out across the valley and it was as if the horizon was further away than it ought to be. I felt that if I projected my will, I could make it further away still. I could make the world go on forever. How much do we identify ourselves with what we perceive in the mirrors of others? I am what Ysobi sees me as. I am what I think he sees me as. The two things are not connected at all, yet I am both. In that moment on the stone, a me in one realm of the many realms of reality sat with his head in his hands, fingers clawing through his hair in the cruellest of despair; in another I was weeping so bitterly my heart was drying out, while in this one, I merely sat with my elbows on my knees, my chin resting in my hands, gazing out over the beauty of an Alba Sulh spring, thinking, *I will not live in pain.*

This will be the long dark summer of the soul.

Lanilsday, Windmoon 10

Ysobi sent me a note. It came in secret, to my workplace, not home. It said this:

> *We got off to a bad start. I'm sorry. As I'm going to be here in Kyme for a while, and this is not a big town, not to mention we share friends, we really do need to be civil with one another. Don't think for one moment I trivialise your feelings. I don't. I just don't feel equipped to deal with them. And yes, I am the hienama and should know. What you don't realise is that what happened was an undoing for both of us. And no matter how much a har like me might like to think he knows himself, there is always a surprise waiting around the corner. Please let us be friends. I'll do what it takes to accomplish that. Just advise me what you can live with.*

I didn't know how to respond. I'd thought he'd back off. After work, once I returned home, I lay for hours on my bed devising scripts in my head. Eventually I just penned a quick note saying, *I need time. Just leave me be for a few days.*

A note came next day to my workplace. *As long as you need...*

By all the dehara, what is happening?

Aloytsday, Windmoon 12

I've shrunk from writing for a couple of days, and I think that is mainly because part of me feels ashamed. The main problem I have with this situation is that there is nohar to speak to about it. Huriel is obviously out of the question because his loyalties are divided. I know all my new friends would just shrug in utter incomprehension and say, 'well, either roon him or tell him where to go. What's the problem?' In fact, they'd probably think there's something wrong with me to be so affected by another har, and by a har like Ysobi at that. I could just imagine confiding in Iscane, who would then be beside himself with curiosity to meet this paragon of harishness who has captured my heart – not, let's be honest, my soul – and then, when faced with the reality he'd probably actually laugh. '*That* is the one?' he'd say. 'You can't be serious.'

I know, as if they were sitting around me now discussing the matter, that my friends would advise me to forget about Ysobi. They'd say it would be easy. Just turn your heart cold. They would suggest some hedonistic and mind-altering activities to help me forget. But the thought of that makes me feel physically sick. I must do some work. It might help.

Agavesday, Windmoon 13

I can't help feeling that the universe is quite excited at the prospect of finding out how far it can push me. I got back from the library today, fully intent on seeing what Rayzie was up to for the evening. I thought maybe we could go for a ride over the meadows and soak up the ambience of the season. We could drink wine beneath the budding oaks, with tender young moths in our hair and talk about life. This plan was squashed somewhat by the fact that when I put my head round Huriel's office door, he had Ysobi with him. *Ah, this must be the keeping us apart plan at work,* I thought bitterly. I muttered a greeting and withdrew but Huriel came after me.

'Gesaril,' he said, 'come back.' He took my hands in his own and adopted an expression of what I took to be concern mixed with some bizarre kind of shy shared humour. I had no idea of how I was expected to interpret that.

'What for?' I asked. 'I'm supposed to keep away from him.'

'You should aim to be friends,' Huriel said. 'It would be healing for you. You must shift your perspective.'

Clearly, Ysobi had been at work on him too. I pulled a sour face. 'Excuse me? Is this a sentence for a crime I've committed unwittingly? Are you mad?'

'You have to get past this, lay the ghosts to rest.'

'His ghosts, you mean?' I pulled my hands from his hold. 'I don't think so, Huriel. You do the soothing. You can tell him I'm a delusional fantasist. That seems to work well.'

'Don't be bitter.'

I laughed. 'I suppose you mean well. You *do* mean well, don't you, Huriel?'

Before he could respond I walked away.

I felt so rattled by this experience, I couldn't face the thought of anyhar's company that evening. I would still have my ride, but alone. The only friend I needed was the landscape itself, unblemished and unbiased.

Huriel has several horses in his stable, and I chose a spirited grey mare for the occasion. She reminded me of the female aspect of the earth, a wild spirit. Her white mane flew in rags over my hands as we raced through the meadows. She bucked a few times, as if to remind me of my place, and how easily she could throw me from the saddle and trample me to death. I'd already been through that, I thought, and then laughed aloud. The sound, as it blew away from me, sounded hollow and somehow sinister. A disembodied laugh on the air that had no humour in it at all. I rode and rode until the night came down. It came right into me. I could ride away, right over the edge of the earth, into a new reality. If the mare galloped fast enough, was that possible?

I brought my mount to a halt upon a high spur of rock. Below sheep were muddled pale dots amid the meadows. A nightjar called out; some spiteful spirit. I wondered about my Nagini spirit and whether if I willed it, he would come to me. Who was he? One of the second generation hidden away in the academy? Had to be, I suppose. He could even be Harua's son. I like to think so.

'If you have wisdom for me,' I said aloud, 'speak now. You kept my feet on the path and I'm walking it. Will you share the journey with me?'

The night seemed to hold its breath around me, but

there was no answering call, either in reality or through the ethers. I might never know the reason he spoke to me that day, or the night he met me on the road. If he had true interest in my situation, surely the contact would be more direct? It was then I wondered whether he'd been real at all, or perhaps just an avatar of Nagarana, conjured from my mind.

From the west, clouds were rolling in across the clear sky. I shuddered; the inexorable change of the elements, light follows dark, calm follows storm. Nothing is ever permanent or certain. Perhaps I had done things to myself, through choice. One thing I have learned: love makes us so wilful. But then I can undo those things, take whatever action I need to protect my damaged being. And I will make the truth known. I will not allow Ysobi to make a fool of me. He must confess. I will say his name aloud into a silent room at least once every day to keep it real. There. I have made this decision. So be it. It is sealed now.

Aghamasday, Ardourmoon 10

Immanion

We have reached the point now where I stopped writing. I truly went into my own dark space of the soul, that long unending night and there were no words inside me. Time has passed since then, and only now am I – this new Gesaril – able to record what the previous version experienced. All I can do is tell it how it happened, albeit coloured by my personal feelings, and let others be the judge of it.

Three days after Ysobi had visited Huriel's house, I came across him in town. I'd taken pains to avoid areas where I thought I might run into him, thinking that this could only serve my purpose better. I had to make him come to me, and maybe he did. Or maybe it was just coincidence. Whatever the truth of it was, when he called my name across the street, I did not ignore him or walk away.

'Can we be something other than enemies?' he asked me.

'I don't know. Can we?'

'I like to think so.'

'What does it matter? You're returning to Jesith soon.'

'Not that soon.' He paused. 'I'll be staying on for some weeks.'

I didn't ask why because I expected I'd get some

partial truth or outright lie in response.

'It will be difficult to avoid each other,' Ysobi said. 'Kyme isn't a big place. Can we not just put the past behind us and be friends? I used to enjoy our discussions. I miss them. There's no reason we can't find that place again, before everything went sour.'

'All right,' I said.

I told myself I would maintain a certain distance in this *friendship*, but it was as if Ysobi could sense that resolve and took great pains to undo it. Every morning and every evening, he would spend an hour at a certain café I frequented regularly and we fell into the habit of meeting at these times. The Cloven Hoof, it was called; perhaps a bad omen. We talked a lot and mostly it was nothing of consequence but Ysobi released just enough of what I secretly wanted. It was the same as it had always been: a lingering glance of far too many seconds, too long to be accidental, a carefully worded comment or question that could be taken two ways; many little tricks that I fell for because I wanted to believe there was hope. He was clever because if I'd ever confronted him over these things, he could simply have denied them. I knew what he was doing, but I could speak of it to nohar, because I wouldn't be believed, or worse they would say I was looking for things that weren't there. But whatever I told myself objectively, I was helplessly in love, while at the same time full of rage, resentment and pain, and a desire to expose him. It was a hideous way to live: an addiction and he the strongest drug.

The night I'd walked away from him in the restaurant was never mentioned, but then Ysobi was adept at projecting an aura of 'nothing has happened'. It was easy to fall into the net. I know he wanted to see me all the time, because our unspoken arrangements were somehow sacrosanct. Both of us always turned up, although the reason for our meetings was never broached. I had to make a lot of difficult excuses for these frequent private get togethers, and I expect Ysobi had to do the same. We did not speak of that. All I wanted was for him to tell me that, yes, he had loved me, perhaps still did, even though we could not be together. I wanted him to tell the world this was so, just to clear my name and restore my belief in myself. I wanted to know that I had not nearly died of a broken heart for nothing. I truly believed that if I was patient, all this would eventually come to pass. Of course, I yearned for more than that, but I wasn't so blind as to think I might get it. I wanted us to be friends of unusual closeness, friends with a bond, but if that was all I could have, there must also be honesty between us. I wanted him to grant me at least some of these requirements, because if he didn't, I wouldn't be able to stop myself doing what I believed had to be done. I really wanted him to stop me.

During our conversations, Jassenah and the harling were never mentioned – well, hardly ever. Sometimes, Jass's name would be used as a weapon. For example, if Ysobi and I were enjoying a particularly intimate chat, where the energy between us was so electric I swear there were sparks in our hair, when I thought that soon he would tell me what he really felt, he would suddenly draw back and start talking about his chesnari. His expression and body posture would become rigid and he would lean away from me. His voice would become clipped, slightly higher in tone. This was always like a punch in the gut, but all I'd do was wobble a little from the impact, smile, and keep talking.

After one such night, he left in such a cold and taciturn mood I seriously thought it presaged the end of our meetings. I was so shocked and frightened by this, I couldn't even weep. But as I walked home, numb in mind and body, a faint voice came to my inner ear through the ethers. *I love you.* I stopped walking and held my breath, my inner senses straining to breaking point. Had I heard that really? Had I? Even the sound of my own blood in my ears was too loud. No other message came. I knew I shouldn't send one back. It would be too much for him. I would accept the crumb I'd been given. It was poor nourishment.

Needless to say, the next day, it was not mentioned. Ysobi was in high spirits and kept touching my arm as we talked, but he avoided personal subjects. When we parted on the steps of the café, I jokingly complained he was too tall to hug and that I always had to stand on tiptoe, or else feel like a child.

He laughed. 'Stand on the top step.'

I did so and he stood beneath me at the bottom. Then we embraced, face to face.

'You see?' he said. 'That is the way.'

'Is this allowed?' I asked him, holding him so tightly, yet at the same time feeling it should be me who pulled away.

He laughed. 'Of course it's allowed. Don't be silly.'

We said nothing more, just held each other for long moments. And it *was* me who pulled away. Had he discovered that trick with Jassenah? I hated to think so.

This toxic situation affected all areas of my life. I couldn't eat, and the only way I could sleep was to get drunk or to take one of the valerian potions Rayzie kept in the larder. He noticed the stocks declined more rapidly than usual, but said nothing. The supply was always there for me when I needed it. I was listless, interested in nothing. My friends bored me. All I lived for were the hours I spent in Ysobi's company, hoping for a good night, more warmth than distance. Sometimes, he obliged me.

'We will always be friends,' he said once. 'No more, no less.'

'I will always love you,' I replied.

He smiled at me, such tenderness. 'I love you as a friend.'

Then when he left me, he would kiss me on the lips, two seconds too long. He would hold me for two seconds too long. And leave me aching, trembling, sick with longing.

Inevitably, Iscane got wind of these meetings and asked me to meet him for a drink one evening. I agreed reluctantly, hoping I could escape his company in time to meet Ysobi. We met in an inn close to where Iscane lived. He bought me a drink and sat with folded arms, observing me speculatively. 'So,' he said. 'Are you going to tell who the mysterious har is with whom you're spending all your time?'

I barely flinched. 'My old teacher,' I told him.

'Ysobi har Jesith,' Iscane said.

I nodded. 'Yes.'

'And he is the reason you hardly socialise anymore?'

I gave Iscane a stare. 'I *do* socialise. What do you mean?'

He held my stare. 'Well, hara have noticed that you leave any gatherings at the same time every night and that a certain hour is off limits. It's the same for breakfast. You never join our gatherings for that now. You're only ever half with us, as if you're just waiting for the time when you can leave. You're withdrawing from us, Ges. And I have to ask: is it worth it?'

Naturally, these remarks kindled anger within me, but I fought to contain it. 'I enjoy talking with him. Sometimes, it's good to share interesting conversation rather than gossip and trivia.'

Iscane's eyes narrowed. 'Ges, be careful. I sense something... dark. This har is weak. No good will come of it.'

'You haven't even met him,' I snapped. 'You can't make such assumptions.'

Iscane reached out to touch me. 'I think I can...' He sighed. 'You won't want my opinion, I know, but you're going to get it. Stop seeing him. It's doing something bad to you.'

From these remarks, I could only deduce that my private life had been the topic of conversation at many of the gatherings I'd left early. 'Thank you for your concern,' I said icily.

Iscane put his head to one side. 'You're going to ignore what I said, aren't you?'

'You don't know him. You're in no position to call him weak or to make prognostications about my future.'

Iscane would not be deterred. 'Think what you like. I only know that a har who can colour your aura that way, affect you so strongly, yet create such confusion and pain, cannot be a har of strength. You're not even rooning him, are you? I can tell, so don't even bother answering that!'

I shrugged. 'We are friends.'

Iscane uttered a wordless cry of exasperation. 'Friends! Hah! The energy whirling round you in that black vortex is not some cosy feeling of friendship. It's frustrated desire and a mournful heart. He must see this too, given his occupation. He's feeding on you, and that's a coward's way. He's doing nothing to help this situation, like, for example getting the hell out of Kyme. He's drawn to you, Gesaril, it's obvious, but I think he's afraid of his feelings. He won't ever give you what you want so badly.'

'Clearly, somehar has been talking,' I said, 'or probably a great many hara.' I was furious but unfortunately not so stupid as to disagree with Iscane's words. He was in fact very accurate in his assessment, and I knew that. But even so, I was addicted and helpless. I didn't want to hear it. I wanted only to hope.

'I don't need to hear talk,' Iscane said firmly. 'I see the evidence before me. Try looking into a mirror, *really* looking...'

I knew that if this conversation continued, Iscane and I would end up arguing really badly. I was aware that his decision to talk to me like this was because he was genuinely concerned. I was also aware that he had good reason to be, but... like I said... love makes you wilful. I stood up, my drink half finished. 'I do appreciate your concern,' I said, in what I hoped sounded like a genuine tone, 'but I have to work this through myself. Please respect that, Iscane. I'm sorry it's discomforting for you to see, but it's my life, and I have to do what I think is best.'

Iscane shook his head. 'You don't know how discomforting it is.' He pursed his lips as if to stem something further he was going to say. After a moment, he said, 'Go to him, then. I'll be here if ever you need me. I just hope you survive this path you've set yourself. I don't think Ysobi cares what happens to you. He cares only about himself.'

I probably shouldn't have told Ysobi what had happened, but I did. When I arrived at our meeting place, he was waiting outside. He could see I was upset, and I confided in him at once. I didn't reveal everything, obviously, but just that a friend had criticised me for seeing him and that they distrusted his motives. If I'd expected sympathy, all I got was anger. 'This har does not know me,' he said coldly. 'If you believe what he says, then I'll leave now. He's just jealous, it's obvious.'

'Jealous?'

'Of course. He knows how you feel about me, the special place I have in your heart, and resents it. How can I defend myself against hara who've never even spoken to me? You clearly set great store by what they say.'

'I don't,' I said. 'I have my own opinions. There isn't a har in the world who can sway them.'

He softened then. 'Come here,' he said, and opened his arms to me.

I fell into them as if into a hostling's arms, my head against his chest. No reason to climb the steps. He enveloped me. A great feeling of security and warmth filled my being. It felt so right to be there. How could he be like this at one time and so distant at another?

As usual, it was me who pulled away first. 'Are you hungry?' I asked him.

'Starving,' he replied. We went into the café.

Our conversation was warm and intimate. I felt sure that soon the dam would break and Ysobi would come to me fully. I could taste it, so close.

The next day, predictably, he was withdrawn and cold. He sent me a note to say he could not make our meetings because he was busy. We had come close, all right. Now came the inevitable reaction and I had to be punished for something he felt.

This was the way of things from that moment onward. Warmth followed by coldness and disdain. Then, when Ysobi felt he'd been distant enough to justify to himself the situation was wholly one-sided – mine – he'd turn up the heat again. It is hardly any wonder I virtually lost my mind. Not only was my heart involved but also my body, and my harish need for aruna. Playing with that was truly playing with fire. Eventually, something was bound to go up in flames.

Rayzie was the scholarly one from the three younger members of our household. He was interested in history and also fascinated by the growth of harish spirituality. Over the weeks following Ysobi's arrival in Kyme, Rayzie was keen to get Ystayne and myself to experiment magically with the various dehara that were being dreamed into being around the world. My Gelaming artist friend, Sabarah, had sent me a book he'd illustrated, which catalogued many of the new dehara, and gave examples of how to work with them. I'd left this book lying around after I'd simply looked at the pictures but Rayzie had picked it up and had devoured the contents greedily. While he became inspired by spiritual images and desires to make magic, I slowly turned into what can only be described as an embittered black ball of dark purposes.

It began one night, as I sat in Huriel's drawing room, moodily drinking wine before the fire before going to my appointment with Ysobi. I noticed that the dehara book was lying on the small table next to my chair. For some moments, I stared at it, drawn to pick it up, yet reluctant to do so. A beautiful face on the cover stared out at me; I didn't even know who it was meant to represent. But I saw a challenge in its gaze. That was the moment I picked up the book again.

I had once fancied myself adept in the arts of influencing reality. I had once tried to cast magic on my rival, Jassenah. Not that it had done much good. We had thrown curses at each other, quite comical really, but what I could see now was that all the energy I'd tried to put into making things right in Jesith – right for myself that is – had been desperate and unfocused, a hot maelstrom of painful feeling cast out into the ethers. It was hardly surprising it hadn't worked. Now, I read what a more experienced and measured har had written about magic. He spoke of balance within the self, of the desire for evolution, of growth. I knew that if I was speaking to this har face to face, he would tell me to cut all ties to Ysobi, because those ties were strangling vines growing tighter with every moment, cutting into my flesh, stifling my breath. He would tell me to cut loose and then forgive. I could see the logic in this, so clearly, but it was as if I gazed upon a white shining path through a locked gate. My nose was pressed to the bars, and I could see the ultimate horizon at the end of the path where it disappeared over a hill, but I was still locked in. Being able to see the path does not necessarily mean you may walk upon it. As clarity settled over me, I became more acutely aware of my pain. I set it before me upon the pages of the book; a diseased and damaged heart. Why was it one har could have so much effect on me? What moment in the universe, what convergence of planets, determined that Ysobi har Jesith could nest like a parasite within me, infecting all aspects of my being? Time should have healed me, but it had not. I was truly cursed, thoroughly haunted. Possessed.

I turned a page. My blackened heart turned to dust and scattered in the air of the room. I saw a word: Mahallatu.

The illustration at once drew my attention. Most of Sabarah's work for the book was executed in flowing lines and subtle colours, but this one was stark and brutal. The Mahallatu were the Twelve and echoed entities in earlier belief systems, as many of the dehara did. They were the archetypal dark riders, who travelled the storm winds and restless clouds to mete out justice and retribution. Their leader was Merim and his eyes were red, his hair the colour of dried blood, almost black but with a hint of meat in its depths. The Mahallatu met in the back room of an inn in a far corner of the etheric realms. In this place, a petitioner could approach them and ask for help.

Within a strange bubble of clarity, I considered my predicament. I was held to Ysobi as surely as if bound to him with chains. If he did not love me, he should let me go, leave Kyme, never speak to me again, but he wouldn't. I was too weak to break away, slowly dying of longing. As others could see my decline, so must he. But even seeing that, he kept me close. He spoke of his contentment with his chesnari and harling, yet here he was in Kyme, meeting me twice every day, as surely addicted as I was. Yet for whatever reason, he would not admit this, nor discuss it. He gorged on my energy, my regard and my passion. He reeled me in, like a fish gasping and convulsing upon the shore, desperate for my element. And occasionally he would give me water, let me breathe, only to drag me to suffocating denial once more.

As I read the text, my gaze flicking constantly to the illustration beside it, I knew that I was about to act. I was about to take back control. Whether this would be a good or bad thing, I did not yet know; all that was important was that I would do it.

I didn't call upon Rayzie or Ystane to help me; this I must do alone. Once I had made the decision, I waited to see whether my Nagini spirit would appear to me again, to offer either encouragement or dissuasion. He had appeared to me at nexus points before, and I opened myself up to his manifestation, but he did not come. That perhaps was a message. This was my time to do with as I willed. The days passed like a dream, unreal. I met with Ysobi as usual, but it was as if I looked upon him through cloudy glass. I ached to touch him yet I hated him. I hated the power he had over me, and the knowledge he had of that power, because I made it so obvious. I was at his beck and call. I never missed a meeting, but then neither did he. What did he get from this? I had no doubt that Jassenah knew nothing about our daily assignations and would be furious if he did. Surely, this constant contact, albeit chaste, was just as much a breach of Jassenah's trust as any aruna we could have taken? Not that I could talk about any of this with Ysobi. The times when I tried to do so were met with cold hostility and withdrawal. So, there was an unspoken pact between us; if I tried to address anything about our friendship directly, it would end. Everything was on his terms. And as the days passed, I drew further away from my friends, until even the invitations began to dry up. I felt that Iscane had given up on me. His concern had been met only with defensive resentment.

Huriel watched me constantly but knew better than to speak. I felt he had betrayed me utterly. I could not trust him. Our relationship had literally cracked down the middle. Huriel did what he could to repair it, and a part of me watched him from the inside, wishing he could be successful. But the fact was that no matter how fond of me this har was, his loyalties did not lie wholly with me. He did not disbelieve me; he just thought what I thought and believed was wrong. Because of this, I tried to hide my inner turmoil from him. I wanted him to think all was well. On a day to day basis, I was pleasant at home. Huriel knew better now than to comment on my social life. He knew Ysobi and I met every day, and how often. Only once did I confront him, when I awoke one morning with a headache that almost blinded me. It interfered with my judgement. At breakfast, Huriel made some innocent remark and suddenly words were coming from my mouth, as if another har controlled my body. 'Are you so blind?' I snapped. 'Why do you think Ysobi meets with me so often?'

Huriel held my gaze, clearly intent on projecting every ounce of serenity he possessed towards me. 'Because he enjoys your company and wants to be friends.'

'You once thought we should stay away from one another.'

Huriel shrugged. 'Kyme is not a big town. You are bound to run into each other here. It's best things are kept civil. I think...'

'Kept civil?' I stood up, so full of anger I felt dizzy. I closed my eyes, swallowed hard, took a breath. The silence was rigid between us. Both of us held our breath.

I opened my eyes. 'You are right,' I said. 'It's best things are kept civil.'

Huriel smiled uncertainly. 'Gesaril...?'

'I'll be late,' I said. 'See you later.'

As I made my way to the library, I was thinking: *you are doing this to yourself. Why are you letting it happen? Stay away from Ysobi. Nothing good can come from this. Stay away...*

How many times had I said that to myself? Uncountable. But perhaps it was in those moments that I finally made the decision to act.

On a chill night of the dark of the moon, I went to Withermoon Copse near town. Of the many woods in the area, this one is not frequented as much as others; its energies are somewhat jarring. Most hara think something terrible must once have happened within its dense hawthorn thickets. I made this visit directly after a meeting with Ysobi so that I rode with his face before me, his scent all around me. I took him with me to this lonely spot. He had spoken that night of how he might soon be leaving Kyme. There was no mention of what would happen to us thereafter. There was no us. There would only be another void. If he'd intended to provoke me into speaking frankly, I hope I disappointed him. I'd mouthed pleasantries that meant nothing: He must be missing home. It had been a long time. So many hienamas for so long must drive a har crazy. We'd laughed about it. He'd looked at me speculatively, that sidelong sapphire gaze. He'd said, 'I'll miss you.' But not enough.

I found a clearing deep within the wood, where a stream ran, hidden by ferns. You could hear its voice but not see it easily. If you drew the ferns aside, the pure water looked black. I took some of this water in a brass bowl and placed it in the centre of the clearing where it could gather starlight. I laid a ring of salt about it. Then I knelt before the bowl. I cut myself with the sharpest blade I'd been able to find in the kitchen, and let my blood fall into the starlit black water. With my blood fell my intentions. I closed my eyes.

I called upon the Mahallatu in my mind. The night was clear, yet I imagined strange, purple clouds, veined with harsh yellow light, drawing in from every quarter. Within the clouds, the malediction of merciless hooves, striking sparks from the air. My heartbeat increased. I could feel them drawing closer, their savage joy. I gave birth to them in the darkness, in that serene glade, beneath an imagined storm.

I knelt with my head bowed, hands plunged between my knees. Then I felt my hair begin to lift in a spirit wind that did not exist in reality. I could feel the Mahallatu circling me, the hooves of their ferocious beasts so close to my fragile flesh. I could feel the rank heat of their breath, hear the jangle of their harness. They created a vortex about me.

'Honoured Mahallatu,' I said aloud. 'I give you my blood. Hear me.'

It was difficult to speak, for the otherworldly wind took the words from my throat; it consumed them. I was afraid because the power and presence of the Mahallatu was so palpable I was sure that if I opened my eyes, I would see them before me. I dared not do that. Other hara had fed these entities with their will and intention; they lived. And even in the state I was in, I knew I must be careful. I would make conditions upon what I would ask.

'If I have been wronged,' I said, 'then may the might of your retribution, and the full might of the cosmos, fall upon the soul of Ysobi har Jesith. Let him be exposed to all for what he is. Make him face the truth of what has befallen us. Let him face the raw reflection of himself.'

I could feel the keen attention of the Mahallatu. This was like food and drink to them. Although the vortex still spun around me, I could feel their stillness within it. They listened. Now I must impose the conditions.

'But if it is I who am wrong,' I said, 'then let no harm befall him. If I am truly held in delusion, I ask that the power of your swords, the weapons of justice, cut this lie from my heart and mind. I ask that I be cleansed to start anew. You have my blood. These are my terms. Ride now and accomplish my bidding!'

In my mind, I saw their leader, Merim, approach me. I could not see the whole of his face, only his burning eyes. 'We hear you,' he said softly. He held out his hand to me, white as bone. 'Ride with me, Gesaril har Kyme.'

I reached out and took his hand. And then in a mind-

173

numbing rush, Merim hauled me onto the saddle before him. The Mahallutu wheeled once more in a circle and then their beasts took off, galloping upon air.

In reality, I swooned upon the forest lawn, but in my mind, in the ethers, I plunged through rushing winds. Merim held me close to him and as we rode, faster and faster, I felt his power spiral within my body, up my spine, exploding in my head. *Come with me, Ysobi,* I pleaded silently. *Ride with me. Let all that is poisoned between us drain away. There is a future, together or not. But let there be truth.*

The Mahallatu uttered unearthly cries. We were riding towards the future, a new reality. Anything was possible.

I think I expected some sudden calamity to fall upon Ysobi, because in my innermost heart I knew I had been wronged. Whatever Ysobi said to Huriel, or to himself for that matter, my instincts and their inner voice would not be silenced. But the days continued as before. I was waiting for a blast of true clarity, the ability to break free. I thought that maybe I would wake one day and be free of the love that ate me from the inside out. Then Ysobi would realise what he'd lost. I was waiting for Ysobi to open up to me, or perhaps to Huriel. Then Huriel would come to me and tell me. But none of these things happened. Perhaps I was too impatient.

Three weeks after I'd summoned the Mahallatu, I decided to revisit them to enquire about their progress. This time, I did not go out to the woods, but lit a ring of candles on the floor in my bedroom. I locked the door to prevent any surprise intrusions and then composed myself within the circle to meditate.

I met with the Twelve in the back room of the inn at the end of all time. The inn was hidden, approached by a single narrow track, within a mighty forest. The trees were in full summer garb, immense and brooding. The horses of the Twelve were tied up outside the inn. The building itself was silent, no merriment within. Dim orange lights gleamed from the diamond-paned windows. I went inside. There was no one to direct me, so I simply walked through the many small rooms of the building until I found the farthest chamber. Here there was a table, and around it sat the Twelve.

I bowed before Merim and told him why I was there. I could see his face now, sharp featured and watchful. His eyes still burned red, as if filled with blood. 'Our work is hampered,' he said.

'By what?'

His companions did not speak to me. Their heads were bowed, faces hidden beneath cowls. Ornamental daggers lay on the table before each of them. Weapons bared.

Merim looked me directly in the eye. My own eyes watered from that smouldering stare. 'Give me a soul,' he said.

A face flashed before my inner eye. Jassenah. His name was a shout in my mind. I knew this was what Merim wanted; my sanction to take his life. For a second, I wavered, considered it. Then I shook my head. 'Don't trick me,' I said. 'I created you. You are an expression of my thoughts and desires. It is I who make the conditions, not you. Therefore, I will not give you a soul. Do my bidding, as I directed you to do.'

Merim laughed at me. 'You don't want Ysobi badly enough,' he said. 'Or you would rid yourself of this impediment.'

'Ysobi is the impediment, not Jassenah,' I replied. 'I wish no ill upon him. Let me make one thing clear. I summoned you not to deliver Ysobi to me, but to make him see things for himself. There is a difference. I have faith in my own truth.'

'You want him to suffer,' Merim said simply. 'Or will you be like him and lie to yourself about that? You have been spurned, yet he continues to play with your heart. He throws it into the air. He throws it against a wall. It bounces back to him. And when he's tired of playing, he leaves it lying in the cold, and goes to commune with his chesnari in the ethers. He doesn't speak of you; of course he doesn't. You are his secret, his sustenance. Your feelings are a fire to him; he is never cold as long as you gaze upon him.' Again, Merim laughed, but I could not speak. Ultimately, Merim was the voice of my heart anyway. 'You desire vengeance,' Merim continued, in a conversational tone. He made a languid gesture with one hand. 'Would not the greatest vengeance be to destroy all that Ysobi has? He could lose everything, even the friends he trusts. If this is what you want, then ask it.'

I had to speak the truth. 'All I will say is this: I want him to suffer as I have suffered. I want him to feel the pain I feel. It is not right that he drifts like a gracious swan through life while his games turn me inside out. It's not fair!'

Since when has life been fair? I hadn't even uttered those words as a child when innocence had been taken from me so brutally. Perhaps now this was my shout against the injustice of what hara can do to one another. Perhaps...

'Let no harm come to Jassenah or the harling,' I said. 'That is the only condition.'

Merim inclined his head. 'As you wish.'

That night I dreamed what happened. I saw Merim gather the Gallatu to him; strange half harish creatures with spiny leathery wings that were like huge attenuated hands with webbed fingers. They did not have ordinary feet either, but claws like carrion birds. Their wild black hair grew all the way down their spines. They were partly like bats and partly like spiders. These beings fawned around Merim, who touched them lightly, smiling down upon them. At his word, they took off in a leathery rustle, diving this way and that up into a night sky, where the moon hung unnaturally large. The Gallatu flew to the house where Ysobi lay asleep. They roosted upon the roof, preening themselves, flexing their wings. They flapped down into Ysobi's dreams. I saw his bed engulfed by them. It was as if they devoured him. Yet in reality, I knew, even as I dreamed myself, that he simply writhed in the clutch of a nightmare. I could see his room in both realities: moonlight fell upon him, clear and cold. His breath steamed upon the air. And shadows flickered in and out of being over his bed.

I knew, because of things I'd learned in Kyme, that humans had been far frailer than Wraeththu. Their bodies had often been unable to combat efficiently hostile organisms that had attacked them. This had resulted in long-standing illness; a thing more or less unknown to harakind and therefore frightening to those of us born after the days of humanity had passed. Also, human bodies could turn upon themselves, in effect creating disease and illness that were merely symptoms of deeper-seated psychological hurts and ailments. I think the latter is what assailed Ysobi, for after the night I dreamed of the Gallatu, he fell ill.

I was first made aware of this because he missed a meeting. Initially, I was filled with anger, fear and the certainty he'd decided no longer to see me. After I'd sat in our meeting place for an hour, my anxiety increasing with every passing moment, I wondered whether I should go to the Ivy House to find out why he hadn't turned up. But then my pride marched in to complain about that. I mustn't. I must resist. So I went through the day in agony, unable to ask anyhar if they knew anything. I thought that perhaps this was the path my magic had taken: the only way to cleanse me of Ysobi was for him to make the decision to end our friendship. I was too weak to do it myself. But when I went home I discovered the truth. Huriel was not there.

Rayzie came to me in the hallway and said, 'Ysobi is... afflicted. Huriel has gone to him.' He looked at me in a knowing kind of way, but perhaps I imagined that.

'Afflicted?' I said. 'In what way?'

Rayzie shrugged. 'He collapsed. From what I heard it is as if his body just sort of... shut down. He can't rise from his bed.'

'How strange,' I said.

'It is,' Rayzie said. 'Huriel is very worried about it. He came home briefly about an hour ago. Will you go to the Ivy House?'

I shook my head. 'No. If Huriel wants me, he'll call for me.'

Rayzie narrowed his eyes a little; they were full of unspoken remarks. 'Dinner will be ready shortly. Would you prefer to eat with Ystayne and I this evening?'

I hesitated. 'No... I have some work I want to do. I'll eat alone, but thank you for thinking of me.'

Rayzie inclined his head. 'As you like, although I believe meal times should be occasions when we forget about work.'

I didn't know whether to feel horrified or elated, although I confess I felt a little of both. Was I responsible for Ysobi's condition or was it merely coincidence? An image of the Gallatu flashed across my inner eye. I saw them crouched upon the roof of Ysobi's residence. Waiting.

Two candles burned upon the table in the dining room, but otherwise the lights were turned off. I did not feel like eating. After Rayzie had brought me a plate of food, I left it to go cold and instead stared out at the garden. So much had happened to me since I'd come to Kyme. My life could have gone in any direction, but the decisions I'd made had driven it along certain courses. If I hadn't cared about what others thought of me, if I'd still been with Malakess, could Ysobi have affected me as strongly? Or would it have all been the same and just created an even bigger mess of my life? How could I tell? What if I'd gone to Immanion? How I wished then that could have been possible. It seemed to me that everything was ruined in Kyme. Just as I'd started to establish myself, Ysobi had come back into my life; this ghost, this haunting. I let him into me to possess me. *I* let it happen. Why?

I pressed my hands hard against my eyes, conscious once more of an ache behind them. An ailing brain. *Let me be free... be free...*

When I lowered my hands, I saw an apparition in the garden, through the glass, beyond the reflection of the candle light. A white shape, motionless. I knew what it was: my Nagini spirit. I'd not seen him for so long. Perhaps I had never really *seen* him and he was just a conjuration of my mind, a representation of my higher self. Had he come in judgement or compassion? I stood up and went to stand close to the window. I could see the pale form, clad in tasselled robes, the face concealed. He watched me. I felt as if he could see right into me. *Come then!* I thought, as loudly as I could. *If you have an opinion to express, then express it. Didn't you guide my feet upon the road that night as I walked to my first meeting here with Ysobi? Didn't you know all that would happen after?*

Then I was looking only at the darkness. Perhaps a trick of the light. There had been nothing there.

Huriel returned to the house just after eleven. He found me in the parlour, where I sat staring into the flames of the fire. It felt like the eve of battle. Outside, in the wind, the sound of hooves, the reek of hot breath, the stink of vengeance. I was numb.

I looked up as Huriel came into the room. I felt that I saw him properly for the first time in ages. He looked tired, worn out. I'd seen pictures of humans; perhaps it was true to say he looked older. He nodded his head abruptly to me in greeting and sat down in the chair opposite mine. 'Would you like a drink?' I asked him.

'Yes please.'

I went to the cupboard where he kept his liquors: all Rayzie's neatly labelled bottles, some with pictures of flowers and birds in his own spidery hand. I took a bottle Rayzie had called 'Forbidden Potion'. A name like this usually meant the alcohol content was potentially lethal. When I removed the stopper, at first a bad smell came out, and then a scent of summer time. I poured Huriel a glass, poured one for myself.

After I'd sat down again, Huriel did not speak for several minutes. I let the time tick by. I wouldn't ask him anything. If I turned to look out through the window, perhaps I'd see my Nagini spirit out there, or perhaps just a reflection of the fire. A log cracked. It was a catalyst.

'Ysobi has fallen into some kind of coma,' Huriel said. 'The phylarch's physicians can't pinpoint the cause, although they presume it's connected with something

way back. Some speak of the legacies of inception –
perhaps death for us is this way, natural death.' He
leaned back in his chair, let his head flop back so that he
stared at the ceiling. 'For some moments, about two
hours ago, he came out of his strange sleep. He raved,
as if in great fear or pain. Eventually, the physicians had
to drug him back to the state he was in before.'

I said nothing, although my heart had begun to beat
faster. I felt nervous.

'Before he succumbed to unconsciousness,' Huriel
said, as if each word was a thorn he had to expel from
his throat, 'he did speak.' Huriel raised his head again,
stared me in the eye. 'He said your name, *Gesaril.*'

I felt guilty about that, there was no mistaking it, but
also gratified. Wasn't this what I'd worked for?

Huriel's gaze kept me skewered. I could not look
away without appearing furtive.

'He reached out his hand as if you stood before him,'
Huriel said. 'I believe he did see you there. He said, "you
must love me. You must always love me. Because that is
the only way I can experience my love for you. Forgive
me for what I did to you."' Huriel rubbed his face,
swallowed. 'A smile came to him, then. It was like a light
inside him. Perhaps you did go to him, part of you did.'

I stood up. 'No! I would never go to him. How dare
he fantasise that I did. He doesn't deserve that respite!'

'Gesaril...?' Huriel appeared confused. He'd
expected me to melt and weep, beg to be taken to see
Ysobi; of this I am sure.

'Don't ask me, Huriel. Whatever is in your mind,
don't you ask me!'

Huriel frowned. 'But... isn't this what you want? You
were right all along. He lied to me. He lied to everyone,
even himself, and let you take the blame. But the truth is
out, as it will always come out. You *should* forgive him

now. Perhaps that is the only thing that will save him –
and yourself, for that matter.'

'And even in this worst of conditions, he still
manipulates me,' I cried. 'If I don't go to him now, and
he should die, hara will say it was because I was cruel
and cold. How ironic.'

'Sit down!' Huriel commanded. 'Sit down, Gesaril.
Listen to me.'

I hesitated then obeyed him, my hands plunged
between my thighs. I felt cornered, threatened, in the
wrong. How could I be? I'd revealed the truth.

'You've seen Ysobi every day virtually since the day
he came here.' Huriel said. 'Why can't you go to him
now?'

'Because this is the time it ends,' I said. 'All I ever
wanted was for him to speak the truth. Now he has. And
I am free.'

I don't know what I expected Huriel to say next but I
certainly did not expect him to droop forward and put
his head in his hands. I could not hear him weeping, but
his shoulders shook. Why was I so hardhearted? I
couldn't even go to him. He wept for that har. Who had
wept for me?

After a minute or so, he spoke. 'I know what he did
to you, Gesaril. I know how he made you into a creature
of stone. And maybe it is too late for him, but don't do
this to yourself.'

'It's too late. It's done.'

Huriel shook his head. He did not bother to wipe
away the tears that fell freely. 'You do not understand
us,' he said hoarsely. 'And we do not understand you…
I'm speaking of the generations. We are still so… so…
infected with what we were before. No matter how
enlightened we strive to be, or tell ourselves we are,
inside ourselves lies a human child. It is not the same for

you. And what concerns me most is that we might unwittingly pass this infection on to our sons – through our actions, our beliefs. What has happened with Ysobi and you is a prime example. I was not blameless. I looked at the situation through human eyes. A relationship between two hara is such a small thing in the scheme of things, and yet it is a reflection of the greatest thing. If we cannot manage our hearts, how can we manage our reality? For this reason, I say to you, Gesaril, do not be consumed by your own hurt and desire for vengeance. Be har, be aware of how, in many ways, you are superior in kind to those who came before you. Go to Ysobi, and release him, as you desire release. Give him your forgiveness. Do not be concerned this will simply give him satisfaction, or let him off the hook. You should see him for what he is: damaged - more so than you ever were, despite the horrors of your childhood.' He sighed. 'I can say no more. I know that I haven't helped you as I could have done. I know that I've regarded this situation as nothing more than the hot desires of a young har getting to know the realms of emotion and aruna. I've thought, oh, he'll grow out of it. That was unfair, and I'm sorry.'

I did not answer for some moments, but then said. 'He must *go*, Huriel. If I do this for you, and for him, he must return to Jesith.'

Huriel nodded. 'I couldn't agree more, but... this isn't just for him and me, Gesaril. It's for you too.'

I laughed and could hear the hollow ring of my bitterness in the sound. 'Oh, make no mistake, Huriel. None of this has been for me. None of it.'

It was the smell of sickness that struck me first; something that we rarely smell. Humans must have lived with this constantly. It isn't so much a physical smell, although I'm sure that in some cases of illness, when the body in some way decayed, then that would have been present, but this… this was a psychic stench. It was the aroma of shattered hope and dreams.

The room was not oppressive; the windows had been thrown open and the fresh scent of the landscape at night sought to fill the air. Candles burned upon nearly every available surface. A hienama with two acolytes had clearly been performing some kind of healing ritual. As I entered the room, he was packing away his paraphernalia into a black cloth, tied with a cord. This har, who I did not know, eyed me stonily. He said nothing to me, but left the room, his two apprentices trailing behind. No doubt he had felt the presence of the Gallatu around this house, heard the scratch of their claws upon the roof shingles and the leathery creak of their wings in the night breeze.

Huriel had mentioned, awkwardly, that Jassenah had been contacted by the most powerful of Kyme's Listeners, those strange hara who seem more at home in the ethers than in reality, and whose task it is to relay psychic information. I took Huriel's remark to mean that the incomparable Jassenah would soon be on his way to Kyme, if he wasn't already. And yet it had my name Ysobi had spoken in his fevered state, not Jassenah's.

Now I was alone with the one who had dismantled my being. I stared at him, wondering if I had ever truly known him. The blankets were pulled up to his chest. He was unclothed, his collarbones stark, like handles. He did not look different, particularly. It wasn't as if he'd been devoured by a wasting sickness. He just looked exhausted. I couldn't find any feeling inside me. I didn't feel angry, sad, shocked, or in love. It was like stepping outside of time.

'Are you awake, Ysobi?' I asked.

He opened his eyes; they looked black in the candle light.

'I see that you are,' I said. I was waiting for the accusation. Perhaps he would beg or plead with me to release him from this curse. Perhaps there would be anger.

'I might be a pioneer,' he said weakly. 'They think this might be the end for us. We don't know. But then, I am young by harish standards. There are others far older than me... can this be death?'

'I don't think it's that,' I said.

He smiled, not looking at me. 'We shall see. But still, there are things that must be said. I have to make peace with myself, just in case.'

'I will listen.'

He gestured for me to sit at the end of the bed and I did so.

'You must understand,' he said, 'that when I met you I had already made up my mind as to how I wanted my life to be. You were an inconvenience, Gesaril. I thought I'd reached a safe place, but then there was you. It wasn't your fault. I couldn't help myself. I wanted to help you, set you on a strong path, but then I wanted to be with you also. I just couldn't admit it, because I believed I was happy. As far as I was concerned, my life was complete.'

'And so you tortured me for it.'

He closed his eyes briefly. 'Not intentionally.'

'You lied to save yourself and your safe life. You threw me away.'

'Yes. I did those things. I didn't want to be...' He swallowed. 'I didn't want to be this isolated creature. I wanted what Jassenah could provide for me. I thought it was right. But then the dehara sent you to tempt me, and I failed. If there was a message, it was telling me that a life of chesnari and harling was not for me, but I wouldn't listen.'

'It could have been so simple,' I said. 'You didn't have to encourage me, or say those things to me. You could have sent me away. Then everything would have been like it had been. Only you waited until you'd torn me to bits, before you turned your back on me.'

'If I'd sent you away,' he said, 'that would only have fed the situation. I felt that I had to let the feelings run their course. I was sure that they would burn themselves out. If you'd left too early, I would have yearned for your presence, and I might have come for you. It seemed better to me to allow the situation to play out in Jesith.'

'That was my heart you were "playing out",' I said. 'My mind.'

'I know,' he said. 'I know that now. At the time, I was simply too consumed with my own feelings. I was actually scared. It made me act irrationally.'

'In all of that, you forgot me,' I said. 'That's almost funny.'

'When you love somehar, and you really don't want to, the feelings become twisted,' he said. 'You start to resent that har, blame him. It is easier that way.'

'So why did you come here? Was it to finish me off? The final act of resentment?'

'I thought enough time had passed.'

'It would never be enough.'

Ysobi sighed deeply, closed his eyes briefly. 'I see that now.' Then he looked at me again. 'We can't be together, Ges. We never could. That is the tragedy.'

'I know.' I paused. 'Why say all this to me now? Is it just because you think you are dying?'

'Mainly, yes. I've lain here and thought about many things. In the midst of my fevers, I saw you here, and you were kind. I don't for one moment expect that kindness in reality. You have every reason to resent me as much as I resent you – this inconvenient love!'

'Isn't part of being har the fact we transcend what our teachers tell us are petty human emotions? How can love ever be inconvenient or wrong?'

'That is for you to find out,' he said. 'For me, I am trapped in the past, despite my training, and all that I've experienced.'

'Love is not just about possession, though. Are we not free to love, with nothing beyond it?'

He closed his eyes briefly. 'Oh, Gesaril... Gesaril... is there any such thing? Can we love without wanting to possess the object of our affections? It is a madness.'

'All I ever wanted from you was acknowledgement,' I said. 'If you had just said the truth to me once, it would have been hard, but I'd have been able to accept it. If you could have told me how you felt but that you'd made the choice to stand by the life you wanted, I would have accepted it in time. What I could not, and cannot, accept is the way you sacrificed me to preserve yourself. You couldn't let me go, yet you pushed me away constantly, as if I was on an elastic string. You could throw me far away, yet I'd be drawn back inexorably. That does not speak of love to me, however inconvenient, merely selfishness. Do you have any idea what it did to me?'

'Tell me,' he said. 'You have that right.'

'I don't really want to any more. I think this is enough.'

'Do you forgive me?'

'No. I could lie, like you do, and say that I have, but I don't want to do that either. I think perhaps it is too soon. Everyhar would tell me that forgiveness is sacred and in giving it I'd rise above the whole sorry mess, but it's not what I feel. I'll never forget you, but I'll never forgive you either.' I paused. 'At least that's how I feel now.'

Ysobi turned his head on the pillow, stared out of the window. 'I don't blame you for that. Be honest with your feelings, Gesaril. Always.'

I couldn't help but laugh. 'Is that more of your teaching? How can you think you can teach others, when you are so messed up yourself? You are the hienama who hara respect and trust. Hara send their sons to you for tuition. What are you passing on to them?'

Ysobi turned his head to look at me again and smiled weakly. 'You might not believe it, but I've asked myself that. One thing this has taught me is that I still have a lot to learn. I suppose I must thank you for that.'

I shook my head. I felt this conversation was pointless. What was done was done. There was still so much to be said, perhaps, but at that time, I hadn't the heart for it. I stood up. 'I'm going now. If it's any comfort, I think you will get better, Ysobi. I think you've brought this illness on yourself. Those twisted feelings turned against you. Now you have spoken the truth, now you are free. Return to Jesith and that life you wanted so badly. You are lucky that it is still there waiting for you.'

'What will you do?' he asked me.

'I have yet to find my safe place,' I said. 'And perhaps that's not what I want, anyway. The universe is immense; I like to think there's more to our existence than a chesnari and a harling in a cosy little community. But that's your choice. I wish you best with it.'

I had been granted what I thought I wanted. I'd said my piece and could walk away with dignity intact. Sometimes, at the end of all conflict, all we can hope for is dignity.

That night I dreamed of Merim. He came to me and

said, 'What you have bidden is done. The Gallatu have flown, the Mahallatu have ridden upon the winds. We found the truth you sought and cut it free with our weapons.'

I thanked him. 'You are free to go now, Merim. Your work is done.'

He hesitated. 'There is only one last thing. I have this for you.'

He brought forth from a pocket of his jacket a slim object wrapped in dark silk. I took it and unwrapped it. I held a beautiful severed hand, the wrist delicate, the fingers long, tapered and artistic. It was Ysobi's hand. 'I cannot take this,' I said.

Merim shrugged. 'It is supposed to come to you. That's all I know. My obligations are complete.'

'But...'

'What you choose to do with it is your choice alone.' He bowed to me. 'Farewell, Gesaril har Kyme. May be the dehara be with you upon your path.'

When he was gone, I stared at the hand. It was warm, supple, as if alive. I held the wrist to my lips and kissed it, in the place where the skin is thinnest.

In my dreamscape, I climbed a grassy mountain that overlooked a valley where there was a lake. The sun was beginning to rise above the peaks in the east. I held Ysobi's hand high, as if it were an extension of myself, reaching for the heavens. Then I hurled it from me, into the lake far below.

In the morning, before Huriel was awake, I went to see Iscane at his apartment, and told him everything. We sat in his dining area, and he listened without commenting. At the end of it, he pulled me to him and held me close. The contact made me weep. For some minutes, we sat like that as I let the feelings pour out of me. Was I cleansed?

'One thing concerns me,' Iscane said. He pushed me away from him, but held on to my shoulders. 'Even though you threw the hand away, the lake where it lies is yours, deep within you. I think perhaps – not yet, but in time – you must retrieve it and give it back to Ysobi.'

I nodded. 'It is all that I have left of him, but yes, you're right.' I sighed. 'This has been a hard lesson, Iscane. I wondered why it happened to me, why so many bad things happened to me. I still don't really know. But one thing I do know for sure is that I can never live a lie. I can never retreat from life into what is safe and secure, scorning anything that is dangerous, adventurous or... alive. I could have done that with Malakess too. He could have been my Jassenah.'

'Don't write to Jassenah again,' Iscane said.

'I won't.' I paused. 'He'll be on his way here...'

'To take Ysobi away,' Iscane said. 'Don't think of it...' He took hold of my hands, shook them a little. 'I think... we need to plan some adventures. As you've said, the world lies before us. There is so much to discover. If you're going to write to anyhar, I suggest it's your friend, Sabarah. We could go to Immanion, if only for a short while, and see what we find there.'

I nodded. 'That's a good idea. I'll do it today.'

By the time I returned home, Huriel had already gone back up to the Ivy House. I had no doubt that he would find Ysobi greatly improved. Soon, Jassenah would arrive in Kyme, or maybe they would send Ysobi back to Jesith before that. Perhaps the two of them would meet half way on the road. As Jassenah threw himself against the har he loved, would Ysobi hesitate for just a moment before returning the embrace? I would never know. And as Iscane would have advised, there was no point wondering about it.

I went to the library and began to compose a letter to Sabarah. Chrysm had also once said I should go to Immanion. I carefully suggested to Sabarah that he should speak to Chrysm about it; see if there was some job, if only temporary, that Iscane and I could do. I didn't want to go alone. The whole idea was too overwhelming. But going to Immanion with Iscane appealed to me. We'd have each other, just as friends. We could do whatever we wanted to do.

Once I'd written the letter, I sat and stared out of the window. Had I really cut myself free from Ysobi? If so, I knew it wouldn't be an instant recovery for me, but at least, whatever happened, I was sure a road of healing lay ahead. The gate to the shining path had opened for me. I was no longer pressed up against the unyielding slats, yearning to pass through.

Was that the end of it? Who can tell? I have been in Immanion for a few years now, and part of me still hopes to see that tall shape in a crowd. In my dreams, Ysobi is free – of his ties, of his own weaknesses - and comes to me. I never did give his hand back to him. I am sure that for some reason, we were meant to meet, but the circumstances and timing were all wrong. I still wonder why it happened to me, or how I could have let it happen to me, when for so much of the time I was fully aware of the folly and toxicity of the situation. The lessons of life are harsh, and sometimes their meaning is not clear for many years.

Two days ago, I was walking in the Lionstar Park, in western Immanion. I go there often to think, although nowadays my thoughts are mostly about my work – the creative projects that Chrysm has appointed me to oversee. It was early in the morning, before breakfast, and a mist from the sea hugged the grass. I came to the central lake, which is surrounded by raised ornamental rocks, where benches have been set, so that hara can rest there to watch the black swans that glide across the water. Somehar sat alone upon one of the benches. At the sight of this figure, I was momentarily annoyed, since I wanted to be alone, but as I drew nearer I saw that it was somehar I knew. Or rather, who I thought I knew. He was gazing upon the misty water, his chin upon his hands, his elbows resting upon his knees. My Nagini spirit. I paused upon the path and held my breath, sure that too strong an exhalation would somehow make him evaporate. But then, clearly sensing my presence, he turned his head towards me. The har was of the Nagini, it was clear, but perhaps I didn't know him at all.

I was compelled to speak. 'Were you in Kyme once, tiahaar?'

The har smiled at me. 'Some time ago. Were you?'

'I was there, yes. Forgive my intrusion, but you appeared familiar to me. I knew a har named Haruah...'

'My hostling,' said the har. 'What a coincidence.'

'Yes... Did we not meet there? I am Gesaril.'

The har frowned. 'I don't believe so. I didn't meet many hara. I was studying. I didn't stay there long.'

I nodded. 'My mistake. I felt I knew you.'

'I look like my hostling. It's most likely that.'

'Most likely.' He did not appear to want to continue the conversation, so reluctantly I began to walk away.

'I'll convey your regards,' he said.

I paused again, turned. 'To your hostling?'

He smiled widely, revealing perfect white teeth. 'Naturally.'

'Thank you. He once advised me well.'

The har nodded. 'I am Lakshmi. Perhaps we will

meet again.'

'I would like that.'

'May Nagarana shine upon your day.'

I bowed my head. 'Upon yours also.'

As I walked away, a soft voice came to me in mind touch. *You can curse a har only so far as he wishes to be cursed.*

I turned again swiftly, but the bench was empty.

Other Immanion Press Titles

Eternal Vigilance
Gabrielle Faust
£11.99 1st edition paperback
9781904853534
IP0083 After a century of Sleep, Tynan Llywelyn has awoken to find the world he once knew utterly obliterated by a brutal war of epic proportions. In a new apocalyptic society, bitterly divided by magic and technology, the Tyst Empire has found that a hundred years of global domination is not enough to sate their thirst for power. They have discovered the secret of the vampire race and have designed a plan to seize their own sinister form of immortality with the help of an ancient vampiric god.

The Phuree, a rebel uprising that has been engaged in a bloody war with the Tyst since the beginning of the new regime, have obtained the knowledge of Lord Cardone's plans and have allied themselves with the remaining Immortal clan. The powerful Phuree oracle, Nahalo, has had a vision that in Tynan alone lies the power to defeat the vampiric god and the dictatorship.

Cast into the midst of a global war between magic and technology, mortals and vampires, in a new world he is still struggling to define, Tynan must make the harrowing decision to save the world he so bitterly detests or stand and watch as humanity is destroyed by a primordial evil beyond all imagining.

"Gabrielle Faust's new book, Eternal Vigilance, is Haiku pumped to the max! You can smell the roses, but first, you feel the prick of the thorns, and you drink the slow, seeping blood. Lock the door, turn off the telephone, pour a glass of fine Cabernet, get the dog next to your chair, and immerse yourself into Faust's world...a 'world that fears silence, a culture that never breathes'. In her world, vampires are romantic, street smart, and, yes, dangerously sexy. Trust me, you will enjoy the trip." – Gary Kent, Director of *L.A. Bad* & Producer of *The House Seven Corpses*

Printed in the United States
132409LV00002B/64/P